This Book is dedicated to many people. My family first and foremost, as you have been here through the entire process. Mom, Dad, Sevan, Angel, Brendan, Grandma, and Grandpa. Thank you for your love, encouragement, inspiration, and support.

To my friends, there are so many of you to name, so this is dedicated to you. Geoff, Olivia, Terri, Robb, Ryan, Sharon, Scott, and all of my friends, far and wide, thank you for your endless support, and many moments of inspiration. I love you all!

To my readers, this is dedicated to you! Never give up on your dreams, and always do what you love. Don't let fear slow you down!

**Game of
Six**

By
Celestial Anne

Chapter 1

"Jeckle! Jeckle!" The crowd chants, as I walk off the stage.

Fourth sold out concert this week, and two more to go. "My man!" My buddy, Kyle, pats me on my back.

All my boys surround me. Some of them are coherent, most of them are drunk. They all pat me on my back as we walk out of the arena through a back door. "That was AWESOME!" I yell, as we make it out the back door.

"Hell yeah it was!" My best friend, Victor exclaims, and I am overwhelmed with head rubs, back pats, and shoulder grabs from all my buddies.

It has been a good year. Three award nominations, and hundreds of concerts. Tonight, however, was my first concert in my hometown since July, so it has been quite the party. All my buddies were there, back stage, cheering me on. A lot of my other friends and family bought tickets for the show. The room was packed with barely any room to stand. I thought for sure, someone was going to get trampled in the mosh pit.

It is humbling to be back in my hometown, and to be able to rock with the people I grew up with. It is a great feeling to make everyone around me proud, but even that won't touch the comfort and peace, I will get when I finally get to sleep in my own bed, next to the love of my life, Kerra.

Donnie, my buddy from elementary school, opens the back door of the limo that my buddies rented for me for the weekend. All my boys pile in the limo, all of them raving about how "sweet" and "kicking" my music is. I get into the limo last, right behind Donnie. I am halfway into the limo, when suddenly my arm is grabbed. "Mr. Jeckle, can I have your autograph?" A brown-haired older gentleman asks, holding out a printed and wrinkled picture of me that Kerra took at a concert last month in New York.

"Absolutely!" I exclaim, reaching out to grab the picture from him. "Who should I make it out to?"

Before the, now extremely excited, guy could answer, Zack, my drunk dick of a friend grabs the picture from my hand and rips it up. "What the fuck Zack!" I yell, trying to stop him as he rips it into a bunch of pieces.

"He's off duty, sorry for your luck!" Zack says, tossing the ripped pieces at the guy.

I push Zack away from the door, pissed off. Zack, who was sitting right in front of me on the bench seat to the right of the door, reaches passed, my pushing arms, and shuts the door. I lean back quickly trying to keep it from shutting, but instead, the door shuts on my finger. "Fuck!" I yell, pushing Zack and shaking my finger which is dripping a large amount of blood. I go to open the door, but Zack pushes me back. Donnie tries to get Zack off me as I swing several punches at him, connecting with two of the four. "Drive." Zack yells, and the limo pulls forward.

"Stop!!" I yell, trying to get up, Zack on top of me, and Donnie wrestling to get him off. "Donnie! Stop the limo!"

Geoff finally gets the drunk bastard of my friend off me, and I look out the window. "Damn it." I say, seeing as we had already pulled away, and were almost out of the parking lot. "Seriously Zack?!" Donnie says, pissed off. "Why do you have to be such a dick?"

"We got people to see!" Zack replies, not caring about how he treated the guy and how much that will come back on me.

"He just wanted a signed picture!" Donnie says, shaking his head, and handing me a towel from above his head for my finger.

"Oh please, celebrities do it all the time!" Zack says, rolling his eyes and grabbing a cup off the counter next to him.

"Not me." I say, watching the disappointed guy out the window.

"What?" Zack asks, looking over at me.

"I'm not like them!" I pause, "I don't treat people like they don't matter, especially in my hometown!"

Zack rolls his eyes again, and says, "Whatever man."

Zack pours a glass of the Jameson whiskey that was sitting on the counter next to him. I look away from the window to see him taking a sip and I smack the glass out of his hand. "What the fuck is wrong with you!" He yells, pissed off.

"You're done." I say, as the limo pulls onto the main road of my hometown.

"Geez man, I'm sorry!" Zack says.

The rest of the ride, everyone is silent. Well, they could have been talking but I wouldn't have noticed because I was lost in thought. Thinking about the guy's face, and how I wish I would have stopped the limo.

My finger had finally stopped bleeding, but it still throbbed and was hard to move. Suddenly, through the anger, a smile came to my face. I began to think about Kerra, excited that I could spend an entire weekend with her uninterrupted. No shows. No work. Just her and I, being able to relax together, in peace. Being able to sleep in, in my house.

My thoughts of the weekend are brought to a halt when the limo stops, and the door swings open in front of me. All of my boys jump out, except Donnie. "You coming, Ike?" Victor asks

I don't answer, because I recognize the face walking toward me in the crowd. "Ike?" Zack says, trying to get my attention.

"Sorry, no." I say, pointing to my wedding ring. "Got to get home, and be with my queen."

"Ewe." Zack says, acting like he's going to throw up.

"She's got you whipped, man." Victor says, patting me on the shoulder.

"Yeah bu-"

"-Mr. Jeckle, can I have your autograph?" the same older gentleman from before asks, interrupting my response to Victor.

"Did you really follow us here?" Victor asks, looking at me for a reaction.

"Mr. Jeckle, can I have your autograph?" the guy repeats, ignoring Vic, this time a bit harsher.

"Of course," I say, a little uneasy that he followed us here, but I'd do anything to make up for Zack's idiocy.

I guess my voice expressed my uneasiness, because Donnie, who has always been my best body guard, moved from the far bench seat on the left of the limo to the seat Zack was sitting on. "Do you have something for me to sign?" I ask, looking at Donnie, who didn't take his eyes off the guy.

"No, bu-"

"Sorry, you have to have something for him to sign." Victor says calmly, sharing Donnie's worry.

"I did but he ripped it up!" The guy says, pointing at Zack.

"I don't have any of my pictures here, my merchandise guys have them, but I can sign your shirt?" I offer, trying to find a way.

"No I want a signed picture!" The guy demands, locking eyes with me.

"I don't have any, I'm sorry." I say, feeling guilty.

"Yes you do!" The guy says, getting a bit agitated.

"Not with me, they are back at the concert venue, but if you-"

"No I'm not going to wait, I want it now!" The man says, aggressively and angrily.

I look at Donnie, who shifts closer to the door, not comfortable with this situation at all. Victor moves to behind the limo door, getting ready to close it just in case he needs to. "He can always mail you one." Donnie says, trying to diffuse the guy's anger.

"No!" The guy says, pissed off. "That's not acceptable, your guy ripped my picture up."

People who are outside of the club start looking over at the guy, as he gets even more angry. Donnie nods at Victor who pushes the door trying to close it. The man slams his hand into the door, causing it to slam open, hitting Victor in the face. I jerk backwards away from the door, and Donnie leans in toward where I was sitting, getting ready to jump on the guy if he needs to. "You need to go!" Donnie says, firmly.

"Please, Mr. Jeckle!" The guy says, coldly, his eyes piercing into mine with anger.

Victor walks up behind the guy, and gently but firmly, grabs the guy's shoulder. The guy swings a punch at Victor, and Donnie jumps out of the limo, taking the guy to the ground. Donnie rolls on the ground with the guy, trying to get him to calm down. The guy swings several punches connecting with Donnie head, but Donnie doesn't seem phased. Donnie wrestles, and gains control of the guy's arms as a crowd begins to swarm the limo. Donnie sits up on the guy, and holds his hands down on the ground. Donnie looks quickly behind him to see Victor standing next to the back door of the limo. "Shut the door." Donnie says, and Victor pushes the door closed.

Donnie gets off the guy and gets him to his feet. I see Geoff say something to the guy, who brushes him pants off. The guy looks at me through the window, and spits at Donnie, before walking away, pissed off. Donnie and the other guys stand guard, as we watch the guy get into his pick-up truck and drive off, squealing his tires. Donnie walks back toward the limo, and high fives Victor before opening the door. "You alright man?" I ask, as Donnie, gets into the limo.

"Oh yeah, I'm great!" Donnie says, sitting down and leaning his head back against the side of the limo. "I could use a drink though!"

Donnie leans over toward the bar. "We'll catch you guys later!" Zack says, as Victor shuts the door.

I flash a peace sign to the guys, as Donnie sets two cups on the counter. He pours both of us a drink, before leaning over to the left and tapping on the back window to let the driver know it's time to go. Donnie hands me my drink before sitting back in the seat. Donnie leans his head back against the darkly tinted window behind him, and lets out a sigh. "That guy is crazy!" I say, with a laugh.

Donnie lets out a quick chuckle and a smile, shaking his head. "You are telling me!" He replies, taking a sip of his drink. "Luckily he hits like a girl!"

I shake my head laughing, and reply with, "I'm pretty sure everyone hits like a girl compared to you!"

Donnie looks at his large arms, and smirks. "Well I can't help it."

He winks, and both of us laugh. I shake my head, as the driver rolls down the back window. "Are we just going back to your house, sir?" The driver asks, looking at me through the rear view mirror.

"Yes, my car is parked there." Donnie answers for me.

"Yes sir, we will arrive in approximately-"

The driver's words were stopped suddenly by the sound of metal crushing. The limo jerks to the right of the road, and I see Donnie launch forward out of his seat, slamming his head into the wooden bar counter in front of him, as I feel myself slam into the door frame. There is a loud screeching sound, as the limo is pushed down the street. Dazed, I look out my window, trying to see what is going on and I watch as the limo is pushed into the side of the small, metal lined bridge. I try to slide away from the limo, as the limo breaks through the metal, and begins to fall down the hill below.

Over and over. Over and over. My body flops like a doll, as the limo tumbles down the hill. I slam my head on everything, as I fly around the back seat of the limo. The bottles on the counter shatter, sending shards of glass all over Donnie, who was knocked out in the first impact, and I. Six, Seven, eight. I try to count how many times the limo flips but every flip brings me closer to unconsciousness. On the ninth flip, I come down on top of the corner of the bar counter, which knocks the air out of my lungs. As the momentum continues to go down, I slam my head into the elevated part of the bar, and I am knocked senseless. After that point, I remember the limo flipping a few more times, and seeing lights as I rose and fell, but I was extremely dazed and my eyes were out of focus.

Suddenly the limo stops, and my body slams down on, what I am guessing is one of the bench seats, before falling to the ground. I lay there trying to regain my focus, but I can't keep my eyes open. I try to move but my body is frozen in pain. Slowly I fall closer to unconsciousness. I lose all of my focus and I see lights flash around me. My head lies down sideways, and I see a black mass move block out the flashing lights above me. "Geoff?" I try to ask, but I don't feel my lips move.

Is that someone's hand on my leg? Is that Geoff laying next to me? My head feels like it is rocking back and forth and my eyelids feel like there is hundreds of pounds of weight on them. I try to lift my eyelids, but they get heavier and heavier. I feel something or someone grab my other leg. Was that a pull? Am I sliding across the floor? Geoff? What's going on? What's that smell? It smells like something is burning, probably the engine. I see a bright flashing light pass by me. I think it was orange, but it could have been red. Is that a fire?

Where's my phone? I need to call Kerra. My body slides again, I think, as I try to look for my phone. My body doesn't move, except the sliding down the limo. The black mass appears in front of me again, and I feel like I am sliding. "Hello?" I try to call, but my body is too weak to move.

Suddenly I get the quick feeling I am falling, before my body hits something hard. My head rocks back violently and the lights turn to black.

Chapter 2

I wake up, my head throbbing, and eyelids heavy. The room around me is pitch black, and I can't see anything but a thin line of light on the ground across the room. I hear what sounds like footsteps coming from the other side of the light I see. I try to move my arms, but both are strapped to a bed like thing that I am laying on. Well not laying, but suspended upright, in the air. Both of my legs are strapped down, and I realize I am not in the hospital.

I begin to panic, my chest tightening in pain, as I struggle to get myself free. I try to pull my left arm up, but the leather strap on my arm keeps it from moving. Where am I?

I look around frantically, as the footsteps I hear, become more defined then stop in front of the bar of light on the ground. Part of the light is blocked out, but what looks like the feet of the person. I yank as hard as I can to free my arms, as there is a loud creak, and the bar of light turns into a blinding wall. I close my eyes, trying to readjust them. I see a shadowy figure walk into the room and stop, closing the loud, creaking door behind it. My eyes struggle to readjust to the lack of light, and I watch as the shadowy figure walks up to me. Its face is covered in a black mask, and its hands have gloves on. "P-" I try to say please, but I realize there is a large object, like a gag ball in my mouth.

The black figure reaches up and grabs my cheeks, firmly and painfully. I cringe trying to get out of the the grasp from the figure. Using the squeezing pressure of the hand on my cheeks, I try to push the gag ball like object out of my mouth, but the shadow man, slams the bottom of my jaw, closing my mouth. I clinch in pain, as the momentum of my jaw makes my head spin in dizziness.

The black figure walks to my left, and picks something up off, what I think is a table or a counter. The object is big and shaped like a box. The shadow man walks back to me, and in his hand, is the object he picked up. With his left hand, he reaches for my head. I move my head, trying t6o keep him from grabbing it, but he gets the side and back of my neck quickly. Using his grasp on the back of my neck, he whips my head downward so I can see the ground. A sharp pain races through my body and I try to lift my head, but his hand firmly holds it down. I feel something hard hit my head. I try to fight as I feel something cold and metallic slide down my cheeks to the middle of my neck. The hand is removed from my neck, and I try to lift my head, but whatever the shadow man put on my head is too heavy.

Suddenly I realize I can't see anything. I look around trying to find the shadow or even just the ground. My head is suddenly whipped upwards, and a loud metal crash echoes, piercing my ears. I hear rustling on the outside of the box, as I try to keep my head up. The rustling stops and I realize my head is no longer falling, but the object is still weighing heavily on my neck.

I can't speak, I can't see, and all I can smell is the metallic smell of the box around my head. I try to use my last sense, to listen to what is going on, but several loud bangs on the metallic box around my head, cause my ears to ring. I cringe as more hits happen. I feel tears fall down my cheeks, as I struggle to get my hands free. I feel something pinch the skin across my chest and arms. Another strap, I suppose.

There are a few more hits on the outside of the box, before there is a ringing left to silence. I think I hear the door creak, and a bit of light leaks into the small space at the base of the box, where my neck is slightly smaller than the hole. After the light, there is complete darkness and silence, as I sit, stand, lay, hang here, trying to get my body free, to no success. I start crying and make the only sound I can with a gag ball in my mouth, a high-pitched scream. The scream echoes through the box, and I am the cause of my cringe this time.

Hours go by. Was it hours? I'm not sure. I try to get out countless ties, but as the minutes, hours, seconds, or whatever go by, my body gets weaker. Even though the straps are holding me up, my body is working to keep my head from slipping down. I let it fall once, just slightly, and the line of the box puts pressure on my neck, making it hard to breathe.

Why am I here? Who is the shadow man? Where is Donnie? Is he okay? Does Kerra know I am here? Countless questions race through my mind as I struggle to figure out what is going on.

My body starts shaking. It shakes in fear, exhaustion, and coldness. I need sleep. I can't keep my eyes open any longer. No, I need to stay awake. Fight Mikeal. If you fall asleep, you will choke yourself.

But I need sleep.

No, you don't!

Yes, my body can't hold itself up any longer.

This battle goes on forever, until my conscious mind out talks my unconscious, and my eyelids are no longer heavy. Hours go by, and still there is no light, no-

Wait what was that? It's nothing, your mind is playing tricks on you.

So, no light, no noise, and the headache causing smell of metal. I fight more to get my arms out, but it is no use and I know that. I try to open my mouth to get the gag ball out, but the box is right under my chin so I can't get my mouth open far enough to push it out.

How long has it been? Are they looking for me? Why am I here? Is Donnie here? Is he okay? Where's Kerra? Who is the shadow man? I scream again, this time the ball goes near my throat, causing me to gag and cough.

My ribs hurt. It feels like they are broken. My throat is sore, and very dry. I need water.

I hear the break of the door, and light footsteps approaching me. I hear rustling on the outside of the box. Something hits the top of my head and rubs down my face. It's a light-colored tube that stands out against the jet-black box around my head. It slides down right in front of my mouth, and something wet starts pouring out of it. Water. Water!

Before I can think, I am trying to get as much of the water into my mouth. What. What is that taste? Is that? Salt. I stop drinking, and start coughing, as the salt burns going down. The tube raises, still pouring the salt filled water down my face. I close my eyes as it passes my nose, trying to keep it from blinding me. The tube stops at my forehead and keeps pouring for several minutes as I struggle to breath as the flow increases. I can feel my heart rate rising as the water continues to keep me from breathing. I cough, the water getting into my nose.

The water stops and the tube is taken out of the box. I feel a pinch on my right arm, as the strap is tightened. There is a bit of rustling on the outside of the box, and I feel a hand pulling on the other straps, some tightening, others staying the same. After a second of silence, there are several loud bangs on the outside of the box. My eyes ring again, and I cringe trying to stop the ringing. While fighting the ringing, I barely hear the creaking and firm shutting of the door.

Now once again, I am in darkness and silence. This time, however, my lips and throat burn, and my nose is running because of the salt water. My throat becomes even more sore, and my hair is dripping more water between my eyes. One drop manages to slip into my right eye, and I cringe as it burns and dries my eye out. I close my eyes and open trying to get the water out of my eye, but another drop of water drips into the same eye, making it worse. I try to shake my head trying to get my hair to move away from my eyes. My hair moves slightly, but not far, as my head doesn't move that much because of the box.

After a few minutes, the pain lessens in my right eye, and I open my right eye. I open it, only to find the darkness like when they are closed. I fight to stay awake as the hours of silence pass by. After hours of trying to keep myself awake in the darkness, I can't take it anymore. I close my eyes, just to rest them for a few minutes. The quick rest of my eyes let me drift into a restless and nightmare filled sleep.

It didn't last long, because my body relaxed slightly, causing it to slide down, just enough to make it hard for me to breathe. The struggle to breathe and lack of oxygen wakes me up. Now I can't see, speak, move, or sleep. Tears fill and fall from my eyes, as I realize I am stuck here, with limited hope of escaping. I cry, scared, and confused about why I am here. I worry about where Donnie is. Did he survive the accident?

My body starts shaking again, and I try to calm it down but the panic grows bigger. I fight to get out one more time, and when it was unsuccessful, I feel my head drop in disappointment. Why am I here?

Chapter 3

Donnie wakes up, and looks around with his eyes, trying to focus them in the bright light. Victor and Zack are sitting next to his hospital bad. "Where am I?" Donnie asks, groggy and weakly.

"The hospital." Zack replies. "You and Ike were in an accident."

Donnie quickly tries to sit up, but is met by a significant task, as pain floods his body. His ribs and head throb violently, causing him to get light headed. Donnie cringes in pain, and lays his head back down on the pillow. He looks to the left to find Zack and Victor looking at him. "Where's Ike? Is he okay?" Donnie asks, worried.

Zack and Victor look at each other, both not sure what to tell Donnie. Their faces cause Donnie to start worrying, and he asks, "He's okay, right?"

"We don't know." Victor says, slowly, his voice filled with pain.

"What do you mean, you don't know?" Donnie asks, his heart rate increasing, as his worry worsens, and he struggles to sit up.

"He wasn't in the limo, when rescuers got down the hill." Zack explains, his voice filled with just as much worry as Donnie is feeling.

"How was he not in the limo?" Donnie asks, forcing himself through the pain into a sitting position.

Donnie moans and cringes in pain, the machine next to him beeping loudly because of his increased heart rate. Doctors and nurses rush into the room, and try to push Donnie back down and he insistently tries to stand up. "Sir, calm down." An older female nurse says, as Donnie continues to fight against them.

"Where's Ike?" Donnie asks, through the pain, as he pushes the doctors hands off of him.

"Don, calm down, man!" Victor says, trying to get him to calm down.

One of the nurses makes Zack and Victor move, as she pulls out a needle. "Is Ike okay?" Donnie asks, looking for Victor and Zack through the now crowd of doctors. "Please, I need to make sure he's okay!" Donnie insists, as he continues to try to sit up.

"We will talk to you about it, but you need to calm down!" the main doctor insists, as the other nurses and doctors manage to lock down Donnie's right arm, just long enough for the nurse who made his best friend's move, to inject him with the medicine in the needle.

Donnie fights for a few more seconds, and then his heart rate drops and he lays down. "I just need to know, that he is okay!" Donnie says, a tear of worry and pain, slides from both of his eyes.

"I know, I know." The doctor says, taking his hands-off Donnie. "Just relax, it will be okay!"

The main doctor rubs his face, as Donnie struggles to stay awake. "Don't fight anymore Donnie, it will be okay." Victor says, watching from the back corner of the room.

Donnie's eyes close, and his heart rate goes back to normal, as he falls into a medically induced sleep. Zack looks at Victor, who shakes his head. Both of the guy's faces tightened with worry for Donnie and Ike. All nine of the doctors and nurses leave the room, most sweating from the struggle to hold Donnie down. Quickly after the nine doctors walk out of the room, Kerra walks in. "What just happened?" she asks, wondering why so many people just left Donnie's room.

"Donnie woke up, and asked about Ike." Zack replies.

"We told him Ike was missing." Victor adds on, looking at Donnie.

"He didn't take it very well." Zack explains, letting out a sigh.

"I didn't think he would!" Kerra says, looking at Donnie who still has sweat rolling down his forehead, even though he is asleep. "Ike and him are like brothers."

Victor nods walking up to Kerra. "Do the police have any leads?"

"They've been looking on the hillside since sunrise this morning, but they haven't found him or anything that could lead to us finding where he went." Kerra responds, struggling to keep herself together.

"Have the-"

"Don't." Kerra demands, interrupting Zack, not wanting to think about her husband being taken by someone, or hurt somewhere without her being with him.

Victor gives Kerra a hug, and she starts crying. "They will find him." He says, holding her tight. "I know they will."

Kerra nods, whipping her tears. "I know, I just don't want to lose him!" Kerra says, stepping away from Victor. I'm going to go help the police look more. It's almost dark, and if he is out there, I don't want him out there for another night." Kerra walks to the door way. "When he wakes up, call me."

Victor and Zack nod, and Kerra walks out of the hospital room and down the hall. "I wonder where he is." Zack says to Victor, who sits back down in the seat next to Donnie's bed.

"I don't know man," Victor says, shaking his head with a sigh. "I don't know."

Chapter 4

"Dosing off to the evening news," I hum the lyrics to a song, trying to keep my mind from falling apart in the silence. It's been hours since he sprayed me with salt and the silence is starting to get to me. I mean, I'm starting to hum country music. Who listens to country music?

Kerra does. She loves it. Knows every word to every song, even if she doesn't like it or its artist. Oh, God, I miss her. I realize that traveling the world on tour has kept us away too much. It pays the bills, but money isn't what it is about. I mean it's nice to be able to take her to Egypt and propose to her in front of the pyramids, but money doesn't take away the pain when she has to go home, and I am out on tour.

A tear trips down my cheek. I move my thumb on my left hand to my ring finger. Where's my ring? That son of a bitch took my ring! A fire is lit inside my tired body and I start to fight to get out of the restraints. I'm going to kill him!

I struggle for several seconds more and then lay my head back against the back of the box. Tears stream down my face, as anger and fear meet. I jerk my body out of anger, trying to get lose, trying to get to Kerra. I should have stayed home last night. I should have held onto her, and not let go. I would be with her right now, if I would have stayed home and taken care of her. I'm so stupid! How could I let this happen?

The door creaks open, making me jump. Footsteps walk up to me, and as the footsteps stop, there are several loud bangs on the outside of the box. I cringe, trying to get lose. "You have a nice body." A cold, menacing male voice says. "Why don't we show it off?"

I feel my shirt rip, as two hands slide down my stomach, pulling all the fabric off. I shiver as the cold air hits my bare chest. I feel a sharp object slide up my shoulders, one by one, cutting the shirt fabric. The sleeves come apart, and both halves of the shirt fall away from my skin, with a light tug from the person on the outside of the box. I cringe as my back touches the ice-cold surface of the thing I am strapped to.

I feel the same sharp object slide down the side of my jeans. I try to fight it off, but the straps keep my legs still. The front of my jeans fall away from my legs, and to the ground. I feel a tug and the back is pulled out from underneath me.

There is a slight hesitation as the two hands grab the sides of my boxers. I feel and firm tug toward where the person is standing and hear the ripping fabric as my boxers are ripped off my body. Chills are sent up my spine, as my bare butt touches the cold, metallic surface behind me.

There are several loud bangs on the head box, then I hear footsteps followed by the creaking door closing. The shadow man leaves, leaving me unable to move, talk, see, and now I'm bare laying in a freezing room.

I shiver, the cold surface and air dropping my core body temperature tremendously. I clinch my fists.

Ouch. Why does that hurt so much? Something must be broken. I can clinch my left fist, but moving my right hand at all sends chills and pain up my arm. I must have broken it in the accident, like my ribs. Once the pain from me moving my fingers stops, I will try to figure out how to keep my bare body warm.

I move all my body parts to keep the blood circulating, but it doesn't seem to work. Is it getting colder in here? I shiver as a cold chill races up my spine. I exhale and inhale trying to keep my body warm, as it gets colder and colder in the room. After a few minutes of moving my body, I exhale and I swear I can see my breath.

My toes become numb, and the rest of my body shivers, trying to fight the cold off. My teeth chatter against the metal chain of the gag ball in my mouth. My chest hurts, as I try to breath in the now freezing air into my lungs. Am I going to freeze to death? How is it getting so cold so quick? I can't feel my fingers! I really can't feel any part of my body. My body starts shaking, uncontrollably, and I lay my head back trying to calm it down.

My head jerks up, as I hear the creaking of the door. Is that water? I hear the sloshing and rocking of some sort of liquid as the footsteps get closer. Suddenly scorching hot water hits my body, and I cringe, letting out a cry of pain. My heart races as my body starts shivering and stinging from the water that is dripping down my body. As fast the footsteps approached, they disappeared followed by the creaking of the door shut, and I am left shaking, as the water on my skin cools off and makes a nice layer of ice on my skin. It gets harder to keep my body warm. I try to shake off as much ice as possible, but it doesn't help my body warm up. For what feels like hours, or possibly days, I fight to keep my body from going completely numb.

The door creaks open again. Again, footsteps walk up to me, and then the scorching hard water is poured on my freezing skin. Again, the footsteps disappear behind the creaking door, and the latch of the door tells me that I am alone in the darkness and silence of my new-found prison. For hours, I shake trying, hopelessly to stay warm. For hours, I try to keep my confidence that I will get out of here, but with every freezing body part, I am left doubting.

Over and over again, the shadow man begins splashing me with scorching hot water, like a sadistic game. Repeatedly I am left naked, freezing, and alone. What feels like days go by of this torture. My body won't stop shaking, even when the temperature in the room heats up, and the shadow man stops pouring water on me. With every shake, my ribs ache and my head throbs. I try to calm down, and get my breathing normal as the temperature rises, but it makes my shaking worse, until I get light headed.

What is this? Why is my stomach queasy? I know I haven't felt good in days, probably from the temperature torture, but this is new. I try to breath, but my head stays light. My head begins to spin, and I can no longer focus on keeping warm. My eyes slowly close, and the darkness gets darker.

Chapter 5

Donnie wakes up, his head still groggy from the drug the nurse gave him. Victor sits up toward him, and says, "Hey dude."

"Hey," Donnie replies, his voice weak and low, as he looks around. Donnie rubs his stiff neck with his left hand, and then looks at Victor, asking, "Did they find him?"

Victor shakes his head, and explains, "Zack went to help them look yesterday, but they haven't found anything on the hill."

Donnie shakes his head, disappointed and feeling guilty for not protecting Ike. Two uniformed police officers walk into the hospital room, and catch the two guys' attentions. "Mr. Owens, we were wondering if we could ask you some questions about a couple nights ago?" the older, gray-haired officer asks Donnie.

"Absolutely, though it is still all a bit groggy." Donnie replies, slowly sitting up against the headrest of the bed, his body stiff.

"That night, after you guys left the stadium, what happened?" the older officer asks, while the younger one looks suspiciously at Donnie.

"We dropped the rest of the boys off at the club, then we headed back toward Ike's house." Donnie explains softly, fighting through the pain in his chest and head.

"Ike?" The younger officer asks looking between Victor and Donnie.

"Mikeal," Victor replies.

"Sorry, that's his nickname." Donnie explains further, looking at the suspicious young officer.

"Okay, so you dropped the boys off. Why didn't you stay?" The older officer asks.

"Wasn't in the clubbing mood." Donnie replies, shrugging his shoulders.

Both officers look at Donnie suspiciously. Donnie looks at Victor, who shares the same confused face and thought as him. "What happened after you dropped the boys off?" The older officer asks.

Now both officers look at Donnie with a suspicious eye, as he replies. "I poured both of us a drink, and a few minutes, I heard a loud crash and the lights went out around me."

Donnie looks between both officers, feeling as though they are going to accuse him of something. "Mr. Owens, do you believe you have anger management issues?" the younger officer, with brown hair, asks, his eyes piercing at Donnie.

"No." Donnie says, knowing where this is going.

"Two months ago, you were detained for beating a guy, who was Ike's relative size, into a coma." The younger officer says with a stern, accusing voice.

Donnie starts tapping his finger on his leg, anxiously, looking between the two officers. "yes, he was trying to assault a young girl at one of Ike's shows, and he had a knife." Donnie explains, with a bit of annoyance and agitation in his voice.

"What did Ike have?" The younger officer asks, making the older officer look over at him.

"What d-"

"Did you get into a fight?" The younger officer asks, pressing on Donnie, as if he was a bad guy.

"What? Absolutely not!" Donnie says, quickly, looking at Victor, who locks eyes with him.

"There was a ton of blood in the limo. Did you and Ike get into it? Did you lose your cool like you did with the guy at the concert?" The younger officer asks, getting close to the right side of Donnie's bed.

Donnie leans away, as he feels pressured. "Absolutely not." Donnie replies, his hands shaking, as he tries to keep the tears away. "Ike is my brother; I would never hurt him."

"Then where is he?" the young officer asks, his cold eyes locked on Donnie.

"I don't know!" Donnie says, getting agitated that they would insinuate that he hurt Ike.

"What did you do to him!?" The younger officer asks, and the older officer grabs his shoulder, keeping him out of Donnie's face.

"I didn't do anything!" Donnie says, his face tense with frustration, fear for Ike, and guilt for not being where ever Ike is.

"Stop Lying!" The younger officer yells, getting into Donnie's face.

The older officer pulls the younger officer back, and whispers, "Chill out."

Victor stands up, and demands, "We are done here."

The officers nod, and the younger officer walks out of the room. "I am sorry for hi-"

"I recognize him, I know they used to be best friends." Donnie says, softly, his hand still trembling, as he tries to fight the emotional war going on inside.

The older officer walks to the door, and turns back around toward Donnie. "If you think of anything, Victor has my card."

Donnie watches the officers leave, his heart monitor beeping repeatedly, as his heart races uncontrollably and his body shakes. "You okay?" Victor asks, looking at Donnie, who's eyes are lost internally.

Victor leans over, trying to get into Donnie's field of view. "Don?" Victor says, concerned.

"I have to get out of here, man. I have to find Ike." Donnie says, slightly glancing up at Victor, his mind racing with the occurrences.

"I will go see what I can do, but I know they will say you need to keep yourself calm." Victor says, looking at Donnie who nods, raising his eyebrows in agreeance.

Victor walks out of the hospital room. Donnie leans his head back against the head board behind him, and exhales heavily. Donnie's head repeats the parts of the accident, it remembers, over and over again. Donnie is overwhelmed with the feelings of guilt, worry, and confusion, with an added pressure of pain. A tear slips to the corner of Donnie's closed eyes, as Donnie tries to mentally figure out what happened to his best friend.

Chapter 6

Just a few moments of warmth and the temperature in the room drops again. My body is weak and cold. The door creaks open, but this time, there are more than one set of footsteps approaching me. The footsteps form a semi-circle around me, as I shiver, my body cold all the way to my bones. One set of footsteps approaches me, and I feel a severe pain resonate from my stomach. I cough, trying to get my breath back, as another set of footsteps gets closer to me, and again something hits me in the stomach.

My eyes water, as I cringe at the pain. My body shivers in the cold, and I try to brace for another hit, as I listen to a third pair of footsteps approach me. Another strike to the stomach, this one much harder than the last two. I cough, the gag ball, makes me cough even more. Another pair of footsteps approach, and my stomach comes to my throat, as I am hit again. One by one, in order, they hit my stomach. Left, Right, Left, Right, each side gets smaller and smaller, as each person approaches me and takes their hit. Was that a crack? Yeah, that's another broken rib.

Please just stop, I beg in my mind, unable to make it out with the gag ball. The footsteps stop moving, but the hits keep coming. All of them must have come up to me, and now they are taking turns crushing my stomach. Was that a laugh? They are enjoying this.

I hear myself cry out in pain, tears flowing out of my eyes. Why me? What do they want from me? Please just let me go!

My body shivers, sending more pain through my stomach and down my legs. Ouch. That punch was much higher than the others, and that was another rib. Please stop!

I hear myself gasp for breath as one of the fists hits me square on the center of my chest. Three more fists hit me; one in the stomach, one right under my rib cage, and the last one was a direct hit on my sternum. Then they stop. I hear the footsteps begin to walk away, all but one.

Suddenly, as soon as my body relaxes just slightly, a long solid object, like a pipe, slams into my chest. I yell in pain, and hear several cracks. I gasp for air, as something hits the right side of the box, causing a deep dent. The hit sends piercing echoes into my eardrums. Something metal hits the floor beneath me, and the footsteps walk away. The door creaks shut, and I am left shaking, my stomach hurting. I try to calm my heart and stop the shaking, but it's no use. I struggle to take light breaths, as my chest is on fire.

Why were there so many of them? What did I do? Why am I here? My mouth is so dry, I need water. Wait, was that a footstep? There's someone in here with me. Please let me go!

I feel something rub along my chest, sending chills down my spine. There is rustling on the top of the box, and I feel something rub down my forehead. It's the same tube as before. It works its way passed the dent in the front of the box, and stops in front of my mouth.

A liquid starts pouring out. My lips quivers as it touches it. A little of it runs into my mouth. It's not salty. Yes! I try to drink as much as I can, my body aching with dehydration. This is so good. I manage to get the tube into my mouth, just to the side of the gag ball. It's so cold. It hurts going down, but it's so worth it.

I ignore the upcoming footsteps, as I focus on getting as much water as I can. My stomach hurts, after a few minutes of me drinking. I can't stop, I'm so thirsty. As I am drinking, I hear a third set of footsteps approach me. Suddenly without warning, there is a firm hit under my rib cage. I choke, spitting out the tube and water that are in my mouth. Another hit, and I begin to feel sick to my stomach. Another hit. Pain fills my body. Another hit. I'm going to be sick. Another hit. I can't breathe. Another hit. Throw up fills my mouth. Another hit. I spit out all the liquid in my mouth out. Another hit. I gasp for breath, and cough, more throw up and water come into my mouth. Another hit. I can feel the ice-cold water from the tube dripping down my body. I shiver, my body trembling uncontrollably. Another hit. The tube rubs across my face, pouring the ice-cold liquid down my cheeks. Another hit.

Salt. The water has become salty, and my chapped lips are burning. The tube is pulled out of the box, and it completely soaks my face in the drying salt that burns every one of my pores. Another hit. I can't feel my toes. Another hit. I try to prepare myself for the next hit, but after several seconds, it doesn't come. The footsteps walk away from me, and the door squeaks close. My eyes close, my body too weak to keep them open. Tears pour down my salt burnt cheeks. Every breath sends pain through my stomach and throat.

Am I dying? Is this it? No. Don't think like that. Stay strong. You must see Kerra again. You have to hold her in her arms. You must make sure Donnie is okay. My body hurts so bad. My ribs are sending piercing pain through my entire body. I know, you hurt Mikeal, but you can't give up. I take a deep breath and chills of pain run down my spine. My head hits the back of the box, and I try to stay conscious.

Who are these guys? Why do they want to hurt me? Is Kerra looking for me? Does she think I'm dead? Is Donnie dead? Where am I?

Thoughts flood my mind again, as I try to relax my battered and bruised body. Wow, I am freezing. I realize the room is still freezing, and my body is shivering uncontrollably. I need sleep. It's okay to close my eyes for a few minutes. Not long, just a few minutes. I feel my body go numb, as my mind drifts into a cold, restless sleep.

Chapter 7

Victor pulls the car to a halt right before the bridge.
Donnie gets out of the car, and walks toward the center
of the bridge, across from the stop sign, where the truck
impacted the limo. Kerra turns and see Donnie. She
quickly walks up to him and wraps her arms tightly
around him. "Hey, baby girl." Donnie, who is a few
years older than Ike and Kerra, says, holding Kerra
tightly against his cracked ribs.

"How are you feeling?" Kerra asks, looking up
at Donnie, who is watching as a crane lifts the severely
mangled limo up the embankment.

"Sore, but I'll be okay." Donnie replies,
distracted by the limo. "Have they found anything yet?"

Donnie looks down at Kerra, who shakes her
head, emotionally. "they are only about half way down
the embankment." Kerra explains, as there is a metallic
bang from the limo being placed on the back of a
rollback.

Donnie walks toward the side of the bridge,
where the limo went over, and sees several orange
vested search and rescue officers moving around the
embankment. Kerra walks up behind him and Donnie

wraps his right arm around her, without looking away from the search team that are connected by rope to the bridge. "How far down did we go?" Donnie asks, looking at all the shrapnel scattered down the side of the hill.

"Almost to the bottom," Kerra answers, pointing to the large pile of metal about 40 feet off the ground.

Donnie sighs, then turns quickly, walking away. "Don, where are you going?" Kerra calls after him.

"To the bottom!" Donnie calls behind him, turning into the tree line at the beginning of the bridge.

Kerra looks at Victor, and both run after him. "Donnie, wait up!" Victor calls, as Kerra and him push their way through the brush after Donnie.

Donnie stops letting them catch up. "How are we getting to the bottom?" Kerra asks Donnie, as they start walking through the brush.

"You remember when Ike and I got our four wheelers stuck?" Donnie asks, glancing at Kerra quickly.

"Yeah?" Kerra replies, confused on what that has to do with getting to the bottom.

"We got them stuck at the bed of the Smith River, which is behind the tree line at the bottom of this hill." Donnie explains. "there's a trail coming up, that takes you down there."

Donnie pushes through a large stack of brush, letting go just in time to hit Victor in the head with a branch. Donnie stops as they walk onto a four-wheeling trail. "This way," Donnie says, briskly walking to the left toward a downward turn.

The three of them walk quickly for a few minutes, before Donnie says, "Ike and I used to ride down here, every night. Right up where is where Ike hit a stump and flew off his ATV when we were in high school."

"That's where the scar on his right arm came from." Kerra says.

Donnie laughs, and says, "Yeah, I never knew an arm could snap like that."

They get to the flat part of the downward slope and there is a split in the road. Donnie points to the left and starts walking that way. "Ike laughed the entire time, as I carried him on my four-wheeler back to the top. Our parents wanted to kill us, but it was so worth it."

Donnie leaves the trail and pushes his way through heavy brush, Victor and Kerra close to his heels. "Here we are!" Donnie says, as they push through to a big clearing.

Kerra looks up and sees the search party above them. She looks down and sees Donnie running up the hill side. "Don, be careful!" Kerra yells, looking at Victor, who shrugs and shakes his head.

Donnie stops next to the large pile of debris. "Kerra, look around you, look for footprints, drag marks, anything." Donnie calls down looking around.

Donnie looks down next to him and sees several footprints walking toward where the limo would have landed. None of them looked suspicious, but something did catch his eye. Drag marks, like someone was dragging their feet as they walked down the embankment. Donnie follows the trail down the hill, and Kerra watches him curiously. "What is it?" Kerra asks, as Donnie follows the trail past them and then stops.

"Something was dragged through here." Donnie says, pointing at the trail.

"It's probably stretcher wheelers from when they grabbed you and the driver." Victor says.

Donnie shakes his head and walks toward the hill. "Stretcher marks are here." Donnie says, pointing at a pair of skinny wheel marks on the ground. "These marks look like drag marks."

"There were two stretchers, and I know they carried the driver down prior to putting him on the stretcher." Kerra explains, shrugging off the marks.

"Then they must have drug something heavy as they came down, or up." Donnie says, not convinced.

"You think…" Victor stops, and looks at the fresh tire marks. "Where does this trail lead?"

"It's probably an old service road that leads to town." Donnie says.

"Ambulance tires, probably, but do you think if someone else was back here that night, they could have caught them?" Victor asks, and Donnie walks over.

"It's a possibility, but I don't want to get in trouble with the police for going out there." Kerra says.

"Well I could use a walk, get some steam out." Donnie says, winking at Kerra, as he walks down the service road.

Victor follows behind Donnie, and after a second of hesitation, Kerra follows them. "Where are we going?" Kerra asks, Donnie who is quickly walking down the dirt road.

"I don't know, I just can't sit around and do nothing." Donnie replies, determined to find something that points to where Ike is.

The dirt road ends at a paved road, and Donnie stops. "What now?" Victor asks, sweating and slightly irritated at the mile walk.

Donnie looks around, and sees a building across the street. Without telling Victor or Kerra, Donnie crosses the street, and walks toward the corner bar. "I could go for a drink!" Victor says, and Kerra glares at him.

The three walk into the bar, and the bartender looks up at Donnie. "Donnie!" he yells, walking out from behind the bar, giving Donnie a hug. "Long time man."

"Yeah long time!" Donnie says, serious.

"Let me get you a drink." The bartender says, walking back behind the bar. "How's traveling the world going?"

The bartender hands Donnie a drink. "Can't man." Donnie says, turning it down.

"Come on it's on the house." The blonde haired, mid thirties bartender insists.

Donnie shakes his head, his face serious and strained. "Why did you come here then?" the bartender asks, looking between Kerra, Victor, and Donnie.

"We need your cameras." Donnie says, stale, his mind determined to bring Ike home.

"Follow me." The bartender says, suspiciously.

They walk through the back-bar door and down the hall. "Why do you need them?" The bartender asks, nosily.

"Got to see if a buddy shows up on them." Donnie says, as they walk into the back room that has only three television screens, a mouse, and keyboard sitting on a wooden desk.

"Speaking of buddies, where's Mr. Jeckle?" the blue-eyed bartender asks, checking Kerra out.

"We don't know. He's missing." Donnie says, sitting down at the desk, and trying to rewind the tapes.

"Oh." The fairly tanned bartender says, watching Kerra, who is bent over Donnie's shoulder.

"This is his wife, Kerra." Donnie says, without looking away from the screen.

"There!" Kerra says, stopping the footage. "This is right as the accident happened." Kerra explained, pushing play on the video.

On the video, there is a small pickup truck, with an orange light flashing on top of it that drives out of the service road, and onto the pavement, driving straight passed the bar. "Just a service truck." Donnie says. "They like to sit back there and take a nap throughout the night and day."

Donnie shrugs and shakes his head as he continues to watch the video. No other vehicles enter or exit the service road after or before when the accident occurred, except about fifteen minutes later, when the police and ambulances showed up. "Just a service truck." Donnie whispers, getting up and walking out of the back room toward the bar.

"Where are you going, Donnie?" Kerra asks, walking out of the back room after him.

"The crash site, he has to be there!" Donnie says, turning in a circle as he walks into the same door that leads to the bar.

"Thanks Brett!" Victor says, as they walk into the bar.

"My pleasure." Brett, the bartender says, watching Donnie and the others walk out of the bar.

Victor hesitates in the door way, and then turns, walking back into the bar. He grabs the glass of whiskey off the bar and drinks it in one gulp. "Wouldn't want to waste it!" Victor says, shrugging before walking out of the bar after Kerra and Donnie.

Chapter 8

My rest was cut short by a burning feeling and the sound of splashing water. I jump as the hot water hits my bruised and cold body. Not this again, I think, as another bucket of burning water is poured onto me. My body tenses, as the heat burns deep into my frozen muscles. Another bucket of water hits me. This one is followed up by a punch to my gut. I hear myself groan, as my battered rib cage ache. Another bucket of water, and another punch to the gut. At least the water is warming my body up. It's not as bad the more they pour, but I won't tell them that. Another bucket of water, and this time three punches are swung in rapid succession.

Why am I so light headed? Just lack of oxygen from the punches. Another bucket of water splashes onto my stomach, but this time it is iced water. Every muscle in my stomach contracts, as three more rapid punches hit my abdomen right under my rib cage. Another ice water bucket, which is followed quickly by another burning hot bucket. My body doesn't know whether to shiver or cringe so it contracts my muscles tightly, as three more rapid punches hit me.

I clinch my fists, cringing at the pain in my right hand. With all my energy, I pull my arm up as another ice-cold bucket of water splashes on me. Come on! I yell mentally, yanking my arm, trying to get out of the strap. I am startled and drop my arm as there are two simultaneous hits on both sides of the box around my head. The metal crunches into my ears. A sharp piece of metal pokes my cheek and I feel a liquid, probably blood run down the side of my face. Before I can recover from the crunching of the metal, a series of punches hit my ribs, causing me to gasp for breath. More hits strike my body, then there is a pause.

Calm your breathing, Mikeal. Slower. Slower. Better. My heart rate drops, just in time for a long bar like object to hit my upper thighs. I feel my stomach drop. Oh, that one hurt. Let's not do that again. No! another hit in the exact same spot. Tears drip down my cheeks. Another hit to my thighs. I hear myself groan in pain through my tightly clenched teeth. Another hit to my thighs, and I lean my head back, the pain nearly intolerable.

You guys don't have to keep doing this. I get it. Well I don't really but if you – FUCK!

Another hit to my thighs and even more tears pour from my eyes. My bottom lip quivers, and I feel my head lean forward, my body too weak to hold it up. My head is quickly thrusted backwards, and slammed into the platform behind me, as there is a strong hit on the front of the box. It's not really a box anymore, more like a metal mask, as thanks to the second hit on the front, all sides are pressed firmly against my face.

What is that liquid? Why does my nose hurt so bad? The liquid runs into my mouth. Blood. Thin, dripping blood, coming from my nose. Is it broken?

There is a third hit on the front of the box. My face takes a lot of the impact, and I hear several cracks.

Well if it wasn't broken then, it is now, I think. I get lightheaded, and my eyes begin to close with the fourth hit. There is a swift and exact hit to my ribs, and that is all I can take. My eyes close and my mind goes blank, as I fall into an unconscious state, my body aching through my dreams.

Chapter 9

Donnie's searches for Ike well into the night. Searching the bushes and trees for any sign of where his best friend went. About one-thirty in the morning, Donnie's phone rings, startling his focus. Donnie pulls out his phone and looks at the phone number, not recognizing it. In light of Ike being missing, he can't miss a call, so after a moment of hesitation, he picks up the phone. "Donnie." He says.

"Are you alone?" A female voice, that sounds like his mom asks, sternly.

"Yes." Donnie replies, confused on why it matters, as he looks at the search and rescue team at the top of the hill above him.

"Seven, Two, Seven, Two, Four, Seven, Two, Five, Four, Eight, Three." The semi-mechanical male voice says, as Donnie tries to memorize the numbers.

"So that is his number, extension three?" Donnie reconfirms, grabbing a sharpie from the tool bag the search team gave him, and writing the number on his hand.

"That is correct. He would love a concert once Ike is found." The less mechanical, female voice says, as Kerra walks up.

"Fantastic, I'll give him a call when we find anything. Thanks, Mom." Donnie says, hanging up the phone, seeing Kerra standing in front of him.

"What was that about?" Kerra asks, curious about Donnie's sudden hang up.

"My dad is on a trip, but wants me to let him know when we find anything." Donnie explains, slipping his phone into his pocket.

"Well it's late, everyone in the day shift is going home, you should too." Kerra says.

Donnie looks up at the search team that is climbing back up the side of the hill and putting their equipment up. "I'm going to stay for a bit longer." Donnie says, pulling his flashlight off his wrist and turning it on.

"Are you sure?" Kerra asks, turning her phone flashlight one.

"Positive. I need to find him." Donnie says, turning toward the trees.

"Me too." Kerra agrees, walking to the other tree line to the right of Donnie. "Me too."

Kerra and Donnie search the trees for countless hours. Three search team shift changes, and still no one has found anything to lead them to where Ike is. "Ike and I were going to fly to New York last night." Kerra says, when Donnie moves closer to her.

"Really? He didn't tell me." Donnie says, looking up at Kerra.

"He surprised me with the tickets the night you guys got in." Kerra explains. "He told me he wanted to take me to the Statue of Liberty, so he could prove I was the most beautiful woman in this nation."

"That's…. Adorably GROSS." Donnie says, with a chuckle.

Kerra laughs, whipping the tears of memories from her eyes. "It really is." Kerra says, her mood lifting a bit.

Two search team members walk up to Donnie and Kerra, who are five yards into the woods. "We are going to search the creek a bit, but the woods have been no help." The young, brown-haired, male searcher says.

"I would wait to search the creek until sunrise." Donnie says, digging through the thick brush that leads to the creek.

"Sir.. It is sunrise." The same searcher replies.

Donnie looks up and sees the sky lightening as the sun comes up over the bridge above. "Oh, so it is." Donnie says, laughing. "Let's go then."

Donnie pushes through the brush, the two searchers and Kerra right behind him. About ten yards more through the trees, the group gets to a small creek bed. The creek is cold and crystal clear. Kerra looks and follows the track of the stream to the creek end, which is stopped by the largest road in this small, Tennessee town. Kerra takes her shoes off, the search team and Donnie still behind her, down the creek more. She steps into the creek, and shivers at the coldness of the water. Kerra looks around in the water, bending down, and sifting through the sand.

Hours go by, and none of the group finds anything. Kerra grabs a hand full of sand right at the edge of the bridge above her. Something shiny catches her eye, as the freshly risen sun reflects in the water. Kerra bends down and picks up a silver and bronze coin, and flips it in her fingers. "Got anything?" Donnie asks, breaking Kerra's concentration and making her jump.

"Not really, just this old coin." Kerra says, handing it to Donnie.

Donnie and Ike are sitting in Paris, under the Eiffel Tower. "You know it will take forever." Donnie says, looking at the beautiful lights of the tower.

"Yeah, but it's nothing we can't handle." Ike says, flipping a coin in his fingers.

"That's true." Donnie says, looking at Ike, who is looking at an object in his hand.

"I'm like this old coin, I'm timeless." Ike says, with a laugh.

Donnie laughs, as there are fireworks around the tower. "Don?" Ike says.

"Yeah?" Donnie replies, his eyes still on the fireworks in the sky.

"Donnie!" Kerra says, shaking Donnie.

"Yeah, sorry. It's a cool coin." Donnie says, his flashback telling him that Ike was here.

Donnie looks at the top of the road above, and quickly climbs to the top. He looks down at Kerra, who is sifting through the sand. "I got something." Donnie says, bending down next to the guard rail.

Kerra looks up, and slowly climbs up the hill, as the search team comes over to them. "What is it?" Kerra asks.

Donnie points to the brown stain on the red guardrail. "Is that blood?" Kerra asks, her heart beginning to race.

"No it's just paint." Donnie says. "What I have is in your hand."

Kerra holds up the coin and Donnie grabs it from her. He puts the coin in his right hand, showing it to the police officer who walked up and Kerra who is still standing next to him. He pulls out a second coin from his pocket, and lays it flat on his left hand. "What is it?" Kerra asks, confused about why Donnie has the same coin as what she just found.

"We each got one in Paris, from a fan, who said we were both timeless souls." Donnie explains, looking at the two coins.

"Oh my God." Kerra gasps, grabbing the coin out of Donnie's hand. "Do you think he was taken?"

Kerra looks at the police officer, who is staring at the coins. "Considering we have not found a body in three days, it is an avenue we are exploring."

Kerra's face drops, and a tear drips down her face. Donnie slips the coin into his pocket, and grabs Kerra into a tight hug. "Who would take him?" Kerra asks, confused and worried.

"I don't know, but when we find out, they won't know what's coming for them." Donnie says, knowing he will find Ike, and kill those who took him.

"Where is he?" Kerra says, the tears in her eyes getting worse.

"I don't know, baby girl." Donnie says, his head on top of Kerra's. "But where ever he is, we will find him. Whoever or whatever has him, we will get. He will be okay."

"How can you be so sure?" Kerra asks, looking up at Donnie, who softly looks down at her.

"I just know." Donnie says, with a slight smile, trying to get Kerra to have more confidence.

Kerra nods and hugs Donnie again. They sit there for several long minutes, as the search team converges on the creek, and starts searching for any more signs of Ike.

Chapter 10

The say silence frees the mind from the strain of the busy world, but silence makes it worse. Freedom from even the slightest sound, makes the mind go crazy. It starts hearing sounds that aren't there, like little footsteps or mice running in the wall. You could talk to yourself to make noise, but you have a gag ball in your mouth that you can't spit out because the box is pressing firmly against the base of your chin. Your mind struggles with the silence, because it is not used to it. It wants sound like your eyes need light.

Just like your brain, your eyes tremble at the thought of eternal darkness. They make shadows appear to be walking in front of though, even though your head is in a tight black box. You see passing lights under your chin. Is that your rescue team? No, it's just your eyes playing tricks on you. Just giving you a hope that isn't there.

After a few hours, your body is trembling on the cold, metallic, hell bed that you are strapped to by five tight straps. For the first few hours, you struggle to get free, burning up every ounce of energy you have in your bruised and broken body. Lack of energy, however, doesn't stop you from fighting, because you perform on stage for thousands of people, every night, and you know how to perform through having no energy. So, you keep fighting. You twist your arms, legs, and aching body, in painful ways to try and get out of the extremely tight straps around your body. It's no use though, you can hardly twist your arms, better yet pull them through the hole that is just slightly smaller than your wrist. You stop fighting. You give up on escaping.

This is where I am right now. Struggling not to completely give up as my cold, bare body lays strapped down by three-inch-thick leather straps. I cough, sending the gag ball into my throat, causing me to cough more, my broken ribs ache, as my lungs inflate and deflate rapidly. I try to think of more ways to get my body out, but my body is too weak to force my way off of this hell bed. I give one more strong yank on my arms and legs, letting out a weak scream in frustration. I collapse back against the cold bed, tears flooding from my eyes. My ribs burn, as I try to keep breathing through the tears.

Why me? Why not Donnie? Why not just kill me?

"They want to break you." I hear a familiar male voice say, catching me off guard.

I try to talk, but it's muffled by the gag ball. "You need to stay strong, Ike." The familiar voice says, as I try to remember who it is. "We can't afford to lose a good person like you in the world."

"Yes we can." Another less positive voice says. "He's useless to us."

"He is one of our greatest allies." The familiar voice says.

Donnie? Get me out of here!

"Are you willing to put your life in his hand?" The not so nice, male voice, that I do not recognize, asks.

"I trust him with my life." Donnie, I think says, sending chills through my body.

We can talk about this, just get me out of here. I wiggle struggling to get free from the straps. "Don't be stupid." The mean male voice says. "He's going to get you killed."

"No, your other people will. He's the best one we have!" The Donnie sounding voice says.

"No he's useless. He's just going to cause us issues." The less supportive voice says. "We need to kill him."

No, let's not do that, I think, as I hear footsteps walking toward me. Let's not kill me.

"Open your eyes, Ike." I hear Donnie say, lowly.

I struggle to get out of the straps. "Open your eyes, Ike!" Donnie says, this time louder and more stern.

My hand raises above my head, and I try to get out of the straps. "Wake UP!" Donnie yells, and it echos around me.

I open my eyes as a bucket of cold water is splashed onto my, now, kneeling body. I look around frantically, and see eight men around me. My arms are now strapped above me, and my ankles are strapped to the same pole. My head hurts, but I'm out of the box. Suddenly I have more energy to fight so I yank on the straps around my hands, as hard as I can, but they do not budge.

"Hello Mikeal, or should I say, Mr. Jeckle" the man from the club says, walking up close to me.

I move my tongue; the gag ball is out. "What do you want?" I ask, angrily and weakly.

"Now don't be like that." The demanding "fan" says, motioning to the beefiest meat head in the group.

The meat head walks up and punches me in the stomach. I moan, coughing through the pain. I swallow the blood that is sitting in my mouth, my throat dehydrated and sore. "Now Mr. Jeckle, do you know why you are here?" The head honcho says, his voice as stale and angry as it was at the club.

"Because, you're an obsessive fan who is a psycho?" I say with a cocky smirk, trying to seem better than I am.

Without a motion from the boss, the big hulk knees me in the chest. I feel my back and ribs hit the pole behind me, and I gasp for breath. "Is that all you got?" I say, smiling, pissed off.

The big knees me again and again. My body drops down, my head close to my kneeling knees, as I try to catch my breath. As I am leaning forward, the hulk takes a cheap shot and kicks me in the head. I sit up, leaning my head against the pole, and I start laughing. The big boy swings back, but stops when the head honcho yells, "That's enough!"

The big beast takes a step toward me. "Matt!" the head guy says, sternly. "That's enough!"

The hulk backs off, and I taunt him, weakly saying, "What's wrong Matty, don't want to get grounded?"

Matt looks at the boss man, then swings, punching me in my left cheek. Yeah, I deserved that one. I wiggle my jaw, and it doesn't pop back into place. "Now, Mr. Jeckle, I will ask you again." The head man, who I will call Pops, pauses, bending down in front of me. "Why are you here?"

I think for a split second before saying, "Because your pussy sons, need a beating toy?"

This was probably not the wisest statements, as Matt picks me up by my neck, and Pops moves away as each of the other six guys, who I will call the silent Six, walk over. They take turns punching me in the stomach. Matt, being the last one, lifts me up to his head level with his left hand, still around my neck, and with his right hand, he swings, one solid punch into my left cheek. Matt drops me, and I land on my knees hard. I lean forward, as far as I could do to try and protect my stomach from any more blows, as I try to catch my breath. My mouth drips with blood on the ground below me, as I struggle to breath. I watch Pops walk up to me, and bend down before lifting my head so he can see my face and eyes. "I will give you one more change." Pops says, grabbing some sort of cloth from the skinniest of the Silent Six. "Why are you here?"

"Go. To. Hell." I say, slowly and weakly, as I am out of breath.

Pops slams the back of my head into the pole that I am strapped to. When I lean my head back down he grabs it, shoving the cloth bag over it. I wiggle my head, trying to keep the bag off of it, but he gets it on, then tightens it around my head. The tightened bag makes it hard for any air to get through to me, and barely any light. I feel a pat on my head. "When you want to talk, we will take it off." Pops says.

I hear all eight sets of footsteps leaving the room, followed shortly by the creaking of the door. I drop my head toward my knees, tears streaming down my face, as I struggle to breathe through the bag and pain. I close my eyes, trying to take shorter breathes so the bag doesn't clamp to my face.

We all start in darkness, and some will end there. I don't know if I will be one of them that do, but my body feels like it wants me to be.

Chapter 11

Donnie rubs his eyes, as he walks into the police department, his sixth glass of coffee in tow. "Hey Don" A blonde, female officer says, walking passed.

"Hey Britt, where's major?" Donnie asks, taking a sip of his coffee.

"He's in his office," Officer Britt says, pointing down the hall.

"Thanks." Donnie says, walking to the other side of the room, Britt checking him out as he does.

Donnie walks down the hall and knocks on the door of Major Brown, the lead investigator on Ike's case. "Come in." A stern, male voice says.

"Hey Donnie," A well dressed, older man with gray hair says, as Donnie walks into his office.

"Hey Major," Donnie says, finishing the last bit of his cup of coffee. "Please tell me you guys have something."

Major Brown looks at his desk, and shakes his head, disappointingly. "We've gone over everything. No vehicle left the crash scene except service vehicles."

Donnie sits down in the chair in front of the Major, setting his empty cup on the desk. "No signs or anything? How does he just disappear?" Donnie asks, tired and worried about Ike.

"Maybe he's still out in the trees, and we aren't seeing him?" The Major says, concerned about how tired Donnie looks.

Donnie rubs his face, stopping with his hands pressed together in front of his mouth. The Major gets up and closes the door that Donnie walked in. "You should get some sleep." The major says, leaning on his desk next to where Donnie is sitting.

"I can't sleep, knowing my best friend is out there somewhere, and his wife is here making herself crazy, trying to find something." Donnie says, irritated and disappointed. "She just wants something, anything to help us find him."

"I know, but at this point we don't have anything." The Major says, calmly.

"How can you not have something?!" Donnie asks, pissed off. "It's been almost a week and a half, and you guys don't have shit!"

Donnie's phone buzzes, but he ignores it as the Major says, "We are doing our bests to bring Ike home, it takes time."

"He might not have time!" Donnie yells, standing up angrily.

"Just calm down Donnie, you kno-"

"Don't tell me to calm down!" Donnie says, tears of anger now running down his face. "He-You-I"

Unable to talk in his anger, Donnie storms out of the major's office, and out of the police department. "Are you okay?" Britt asks, concerned, as she walks back inside.

Donnie shakes his head, pissed off, walking straight to his car. He gets into his car and punches the steering wheel several times, angrily, tears rolling down his face. After a few minutes, Donnie calms down, and pulls out his phone. On his phone, there is a text message from an unknown number. "Just a service truck." The number says.

Donnie looks curiously at the message. His phone buzzes in his hand again, as another text message from the same number comes in. "Things are not always as they seem."

"Who is this?" Donnie texts the number back.

"A friend." The number replies.

Donnie looks suspiciously at his phone intensely reading the messages repeatedly. There is a knock at the window, and Donnie jumps. He looks and it's Britt. He rolls down the window, and Britt leans in. "Hey, are you okay?" Britt asks, leaning over the window, her head on her arms.

"Yeah, just a bit overwhelmed with all of this." Donnie says, rubbing his neck and setting his phone down in the center console.

"My shift ends in an hour, do you want to get a drink?" Britt asks, with a warm smile.

Donnie sighs. He shrugs then nods his head. "Yeah, I could use a drink." Donnie replies, his mind more focused on the text messages than Britt.

"Good. Meet me at Henry's at, say, 6:15?" Britt says, standing up from Donnie's car.

Donnie nods and Britt smiles, walking back toward the police department. Donnie turns on his small four door car, and leaves the police department, driving back to Ike's house. Donnie pulls into the driveway, and Kerra's car isn't there. He walks inside, using the key Kerra and Ike gave him last year before they went on tour. Donnie goes to the kitchen and finds a note on the counter. "Hey Don, went to do something with the police. I will be back later, there's food in the fridge, if you are hungry. Love, Kerra."

Donnie nods, rubbing his exhausted eyes, and walking to the fridge. Donnie opens the fridge and pulls his phone out of his pocket. He dials the number his mom gave him a few nights ago. "Sorry the number you have reached has been disconnected, please try again later." The automatic phone voice says, and Donnie hangs up.

He redials, thinking he miscalled a number, because it is wearing off of his hand. "Sorry the number you have reached has been disconnected, please try again later." The automatic phone voice repeats, and Donnie hangs up, confused.

He calls his mom. "Hey sweetie, how are you?" a warm, female voice says, answering the phone.

"Hey mom, I've been a lot better." Donnie says. "but hey, they number you gave me for dad, isn't working."

"What number?" His mom asks, confused.

"He's on a trip." Donnie replies, just as confused as his mom. "You texted and called a few nights ago."

There is a pause then Donnie's mom, who is concerned, replies, "Sweetie, your dad is here with me, he has been all week."

"Hey son." A male voice says.

"What?" Donnie asks, confused. "You didn't call or text me?"

"No sweetheart. When was the last time you slept?" Donnie's mom's concern voice replies.

"A few days ago, I think." Donnie says, closing the fridge, and putting his hand on his head, beyond confused.

"Get some rest honey, you're not making any sense." His mom says, concerned for the well being of her son.

"Yeah, I will." Donnie says, his mind distracted and confused. "Love you."

Donnie hangs up the phone, and looks through the call log to see the numbers who have called in the past few days. "What is going on?" Donnie asks, mumbling to himself.

Donnie shakes his head, opening the fridge, as his phone buzzes on the counter. "Things are not as they seem." A text message comes through, from the same number as earlier.

"What does that mean?" Donnie asks himself, confused and aggravated.

The text comes in again. Donnie's phone starts going nuts, as the text comes in repeatedly. Donnie looks at his phone, trying to make it stop. "I get it!" Donnie yells, as his phone freezes, because of the rapidness of the texts.

His phone vibrates uncontrollably, and he yells, "Stop!"

Donnie takes his battery out, and turns it back on, trying to get it to stop. It turns on and unlocks, but as soon as he clicks on the text message bubble at the bottom of its screen, the phone starts vibrating and new text messages start flooding in again. Donnie looks at it and tries to hit the home button, but the messages don't go away. Donnie sets his phone on the counter, trying to wait to see if it will stop. Twenty minutes go by and his phone is still blowing up. He takes the battery out several more times, and it doesn't seem to work. Thousands of the same message floods his phone, and he begins to get aggravated. He hits every button, resets his phone, and the text messages continue to come. Finally, Donnie has had enough. "I get it!" Donnie yells, throwing his phone at the wall, shattering it all over the floor in the kitchen. Donnie grabs his car keys off the counter, and leaves, slamming the door behind him.

Chapter 12

In. Out. In Out. I try to slow my breathing as much as I can to keep the bag from restricting my neck too much. Is it time to go home yet? I want to. I don't want to be here. I want to see my beautiful wife. I want to make sure Donnie is okay. I just have to get out of these restraints first. I yank on my arm restraints, and they get tighter around my wrists. Come on! Let go!

I push with my ankles, and yank on my arms, trying to get the restraints to break. They don't budge, except digging deeper into my wrists. Damn it! I drop down releasing the pressure. I start whistling, tears in my eyes, and blood dripping off my fingertips.

It's been days since I've been here, and I just want to go home. Why did they take me? I yank on my arms and I feel a large pop in my shoulder. The cuts on my wrists from the restraints open more. I lean back toward the pole, releasing the pressure again. I slide my hands down the pole and grab a hold of the restraints on my legs. I pull up, trying to snap the bands. Instead of snapping the bands, my hand slips and I hear a snap as the pink finger on my left-hand bends back and snaps at the knuckle. "Fuck" I mumble to myself, as pain shoots through my hand and I sit down on my ankles.

This weekend was not supposed to happen like this. Kerra and I were supposed to fly to New York. I was going to surprise her with Phantom of the Opera tickets, and a new diamond necklace I bought in Italy. It was going to be a romantic weekend and it would show her that she is the most beautiful lady in the world. How could I let this happen? Who are these guys? Is Donnie okay? Are my boys okay? This psycho won't and can't win. I need to make it back for my family, my friends, and my fans. My alpha team six.

The door creaks open, and only one set of footsteps walk in. the footsteps walk up to me, and I prepare to be hit, but the steps walk right by me. A few seconds go by and I hear a second set of footsteps walk in and walk to my left, stopping next to me. The footsteps continue to come in, each stopping at various points around me to form an eight-point circle. "Pick a number between 1 and 8." I hear the prick says.

"I don't gamble." I say, still very weak and hungry.

"I said pick a number!" The head bitch says, as a fist connects with my lower jaw.

"Nine," I say adding the two odds.

Another fist connects with the other side of my jaw, and I cringe, feeling my jaw pop farther out of place. "Pick a number between one and eight!" The tutu wearing boss man says.

"Two and Three-fourths." I say, knowing whatever the other numbers are, are worse than getting punched.

"Fine, you worthless trash. You get eight." The easily angered man in charge says, as a surge of electricity is sent through my body.

All of my muscles lock and my lungs quickly deflate. I shake, feeling the worst pain I have ever felt in my life. The electricity stops, and I fall down, my body, now weaker than it was. Without a word, another surge of electricity goes through my body. I hear a scream. Was that me? My muscle contract, and I feel like I'm going to die. Maybe I should have picked a number. The electricity stops and I collapse again, onto the ground, well as far I can do with my arms strapped behind me.

I take several quick and deep breaths, my entire body tingling. My pain senses are tingling uncontrollably. "Pick a number between one and eight." The fire breathing puppet master says, as I listen to the footsteps walk around the room.

"Seven." I say, hoping it's easier than electricity.

Boy, was I wrong. The bag is yanked from my head, and my head is leaned backwards toward the pole behind me. The hulk man rips open my jaw, which pops, sending pain through my entire head. They pour salt water not my mouth, them shove my jaw closed, pinching my nose. I try to spit it out, but they hold my jaw shut strongly until I swallow the water. Too weak to fight my jaw to stay closed, the hulk pulls it open again and they pour more salt water in. My throat burns and my eyes water, as I fight not to have to swallow it. This time the hulk punches my stomach and I swallow. One more time they open my mouth, pouring water in. They hold my mouth and nose shut until I swallow it.

The hulk man puts the bag back over my head, and I drop down, exhausted, and now even more thirsty than I was. Now for those of you wondering why I say salt water is worse than electricity. If you are electrocuted the feeling fades, but salt dehydrates you completely, especially when you are already dehydrated. Wait what number did I pick? Did I pick a number?

A rope wraps around my throat. I drop my chin, as it pulls my head against the pole. I use my chin to fight the rope, but I feel fingers push against my closed chin. My jaw aches as I fight to keep my chin down, against the opposing fingers. I feel the rope fall away from my chin, then raise, slipping under my fighting jaw. I gasp, the rope cutting off the oxygen in my body.

Well this is it. I can't survive if I can't breathe. I'm going to die. My hands are tied behind my back so I can't pull the rope off. I start to fight off unconsciousness, as my head gets light due to lack of oxygen. I feel my eyes close, and the next second, I am laying on a concrete floor, hands by my side, but connected on the ground by metal chains. I attempt to sit up, but my body is too weak. I couch, my throat dryer than a desert and the bruising on my ribs are almost as dark as the night sky. I use my right elbow to roll onto my left hip.

I cough my ribs stinging in pain. I watch, my eyes having trouble focusing, as a figure bends down in front of me. I open my eyes as wide as I can, and they start to focus. Kneeling in front of me is the head honcho, and behind him stands his six-seven wall that broke my jaw. "Please," I mumble, barely audible.

I can't move my body. I am too tired. I try to sit up but my arms collapse, and I end back at the positive I was in. "Please." I beg, using all of my remaining energy to get the word out.

I feel a tear slide down my cheek, as I try to sit up again. The head honcho pushes me back down to the ground. I lay there looking at him, weak, tired, and crying. "Please." I beg again, terrified and wanting them to let me go.

"We will let you go," the head pain in my ass says, leaning closer to me. "But first-"

"We're going to play a game!" the silent six says in a chorus like voice.

I look at them confused, and the hulk kicks me in the head, knocking the lights completely out.

Chapter 13

Donnie gets to the bar at a quarter to five o'clock, and immediately orders a beer. The bartender hands him a beer and Donnie walks to the far booth in the corner of the building, away from everyone. He sits at the table, drinking his beer quickly, as he stares blank faced, at the seat in front of him. He covers his face, trying to keep himself awake and calm. There is a sound of glass clanging next to Donnie and he looks up to the bartender who sets two beers on the table in front of him. "On the house!" The bar owner and tender, Henry, who went to school with Donnie and Ike, says.

Henry sets the ice bucket on the table, putting the second been in it next to two others. "Those are from Mikey." Henry says, and Donnie looks up to see Mikey sitting at the bar holding up his beer. Donnie lifts his new beer, then takes a big gulp of it. Henry goes back to work, leaving Donnie to drink his beers alone.

Time ticks by, and Donnie slides his feet onto the seat in front of him, and leans his head against the wall behind him. He takes a sip of his fourth beer, and closes his eyes. He tries to get the feeling of responsibility to leave his mind, but it doesn't want to. It's a quarter till seven, but Donnie doesn't seem to care. He takes another drink of his beer, and finishes it off. Donnie leans forward, and grabs his fifth beer. He doesn't move from that position, however, as the television catches his attention. It's a news cast about Ike. Donnie freezes, his face tight, trying not to let the overwhelming sense of guilt come back. The subtitles flash across the screen, as the news reporter talks about the accident and Ike's legacy, as if he is dead.

A tear drips down his face, as Britt walks into the bar. Henry points to Donnie, and she walks over. "Sorry, I'm late." Britt says, but Donnie doesn't acknowledge her presence. "I see you started before me." Britt teases with a laugh, as she moves several empty beer bottles.

Donnie is still locked onto the story, his face getting redder, as he tries to fight back the emotions. Britt looks at Donnie and notices something isn't right. "Hey, are you okay?" Britt asks, putting her hand on his, as Henry changes the channel to football.

Donnie looks at Britt, tears sitting in his eyes. "You okay?" Britt asks, concerned.

Donnie nods, drinking the entirety of his fifth beer. "They'll find him!" Britt says, trying to comfort Donnie.

Britt looks at Donnie's hand and sees it is shaking. Henry sets several more beers in front of Donnie, and a glass of whiskey. Donnie looks at Britt, and he closes his fist on his right hand, stopping it from shaking. "Sorry." He says, his voice stiff.

"It's okay, you are going through a lot." Britt says, and Donnie drinks his entire glass of whiskey.

"How was your day?" Donnie asks, trying to divert the situation, his voice still filled with strain.

Henry sets a margarita in front of Britt, as she replies, "Good, but long!" Britt takes a drink of her margarita then explains, "Some crazy locked his family in a basement, that's why I was late."

"Sounds like a downstairs story." Donnie says, with a smile and chuckle.

Britt nearly spits her sip of margarita out, as she laughs, caught off guard by Donnie's joke. "That was so lame!" Britt says, making Donnie laugh more.

"I know." Donnie says, both laughing.

"Do you guys need something to eat?" Henry asks.

"Do you like wings?" Donnie asks Britt, realizing he hasn't eaten anything all day.

"Absolutely!" Britt says, excited.

"So Wings?" Henry says.

"And cheese fries!" Donnie says, and Britt nods in agreeance.

Donnie hands Henry his credit card. "Just put it all on this." Donnie says, and Henry walks away.

"So do you work tomorrow?" Donnie asks, taking a sip of the ice cold beer.

"No, it's my day off." Britt says, sipping her margarita.

"In that case." Donnie pauses, looking at the bar. "Henry, can we have two shots of Don Julio please?"

"Coming right up!" Henry hollers back, finishing their order of wings.

Henry sets the wings down, and hands Donnie and Britt their shots. "Enjoy!" Henry says, setting a bottle of ranch at the edge of the table, before walking away.

"To Ike, may he come home safely!" Britt says, holding her glass up.

Donnie smiles and nods, meeting his glass with her. "Safe and sound." Donnie adds on, before taking his shot.

They laugh and talk all night, Ike still at the back of Donnie's mind. At a quarter to midnight, they walk out of the bar, Donnie a bit drunk, and get into a cab. Still talking and laughing, they ride to Britt's house, which is just up the road. Donnie smiles, and looks out the cab window, just in time to see the shattered and jagged guardrail where the limo was shoved through. His jaw line tightens, as even the alcohol isn't strong enough to fight off the feelings of worry and self-blame. Britt grabs his hand, and Donnie turns, faking a smile, trying not to let her see he is hurting. "You okay?" Britt asks, seeing right through his fake smile.

Donnie nods in response as the cab turns down a road, stopping at the end of Britt's driveway. Britt hands the cab driver the fee before crawling out of the back seat, after Donnie who stumbles a bit when he stands up. "Nice house." Donnie says, swaying a bit, as they walk up the long driveway.

"It's small, but nice!" Britt says, holding Donnie's arm, as they walk toward the front door.

Britt opens the door and Donnie follows her in. "Woah! It's bigger on the inside." Donnie exclaims teasing Britt.

"What were you expecting?" Britt asks, with a laugh, watching him sway as he walks around the room.

"Like... A Box!" Donnie says, laughing with a wink.

Britt pushes him in the arm, laughing. "You aren't right!" Britt says, her eyes tearing up from laughing so much.

Donnie sticks his tongue out, still laughing as he leans against the wall, trying to keep himself up. Britt realizes that Donnie's laugh is stiff with pain. "Oh really?" Britt says, coming up to Donnie. Donnie grabs her, and tickles her hips. "No!" Britt yells, turning to get away from him.

Donnie grabs her, and turns her against the wall of the hallway. Donnie smiles through the pain, his hands on her hips. Britt locks eyes with him, as he leans in for a kiss. Both of their eyes close, as they kiss. Britt puts her arms around Donnie's neck, as he lifts her into his arms, their lips locked. Donnie runs his hands up her back pulling her shirt with them, as he drunkenly walks toward Britt's bedroom, their lips still locked.

Britt slips Donnie shirt off, and drops it in the doorway, as they walk through. Donnie gently lays Britt on the mattress, crawling on after her, kissing her neck then her lips. They kiss for several minutes, as Donnie rubs Britt's sides and chest softly. Britt rolls Donnie onto the mattress, straddling him. She unstraps her bra, throwing it onto the ground, before leaning in for another kiss. Britt rubs her hand up Donnie's stomach onto his chest, as they kiss. As she rubs passed his ribs, she feels his stomach tighten, but he doesn't miss a kiss. Broken ribs from the accident, she assumes, moving her hands around his neck, still kissing him. He leans in kissing her neck and chest, for a moment the worries disappear from his mind.

It is short lived, as a car passes and the light reflects off the mirrors, illumining the room. Donnie stops as more lights reflect around the room quickly. There is a bang outside, and Donnie's head shoots toward the windows. Flashbacks from the accident start.

Donnie is thrown forward as there is a loud crashing sound. He hears Ike say, "Shit!" as his head hits something hard and he is knocked into a daze. Donnie hears glass bottles shattering around him, as he is thrown around the flipping limo. The sound of crushing metal fills the air, as the limo careens down the rocky embankment. Donnie's head hits something hard, and he is knocked closer to unconsciousness, as his body flops around like a rag doll in the hands of a three-year-old. "Is that Ike?" the nearly unconscious Donnie thinks, as he lands on a large mass. The limo flips again, slamming Donnie against the counter again, knocking him completely unconscious.

Donnie opens his eyes, his body sweating profusely as his heart races. He sits up to see Britt kneeled on the in front of him, softly holding both of his hands, concerned. He feels a tear roll down his cheek and she wraps him in a tight, but soft hug. "I'm sorry." Donnie whispers, crying, his entire body trembling.

"Don't be. It's not your fault." Britt says, holding him. "You've held it strong, but even the strongest warriors have their moments of weakness."

Donnie squeezes Britt, his cheeks becoming soaked with tears, as all the emotions of recent events sober him up. They sit hugging each other for several long minutes, and Britt rubs Donnie's tense and bare back. Donnie starts shivering, his bare feet sitting on the cold ground in front of the bed. "Here," Britt says, standing up and handing him his t-shirt.

Donnie puts his shirt on, and slides up the bed, laying down. Britt crawls into bed next to him, pulling the covers over them before wrapping her left hand over his stomach. Donnie grabs her hand, and stares up at the ceiling. After about an hour of watching Donnie, Britt falls asleep, and Donnie continues to lay there, his mind racing with the overwhelming emotions of the accident.

After a while of lying there awake, Donnie leans over and kisses Britt on the forehead. He gets up, slipping his shoes on, before leaving. Donnie slips his hands in his jeans' pockets, as he walks down Britt's driveway in the brisk early morning air.

Donnie walks down the street toward the bridge, his arms burning from the chilled wind. Donnie stops in the middle of the bridge, where the limo went over the edge. He turns around and watches as the truck drives passed the stop sign, and slams directly into the driver's door of the limo. Donnie shakes his head trying to get the thoughts out of his head. Donnie sits down on the edge of the concrete, his legs hanging over the embankment, as he watches the limo tumble down the rocks below. He can smell the burning of the asphalt from the truck's tires, and can hear the echoing sound of metal crushing in on his and Ike's bodies. "Where did you go?" Donnie whispers to Ike, as the limo stops moving.

Donnie remembers the text from the unknown number, and remembers the video from the bar. "It's not what it seems?" Donnie whispers to himself. "Oh my God."

Donnie jumps up, nearly running into a slow passing car, who honks, scaring him. Donnie follows the car swiftly, trying to get to Ike's house, before Kerra leaves for the police department. The car stops and reverses toward Donnie slowly. Donnie moves to the side of the road, and the car stops next to him. "Hey Don. Need a ride?" Henry, the bartender from the night before asks.

"You heading to work?" Donnie says, his arms cold.

"You know it. Well I forgot my wallet, so I have to run back." Henry says, with a laugh.

"Sweet, yeah man. Thanks!" Donnie says, getting in the passenger seat.

"No problem." Henry says, driving toward the bar.

Chapter 14

A game, they say. Games are supposed to be fun. I have a feeling that this game will be far from fun. The hulk stands me up, taking my chains off. My legs shake, barely able to carry the weight of my body as he pushes me toward the creaking door. I stumble, falling to my knees. The muscle man kicks me in the stomach and I gasp for breath, rolling onto my back. He goes for another kick, but stops, as the puppet king yells, "Stop!"

The walking dumbbell, with an emphasis on the dumb part, lifts me back to my feet. The ice cold concrete sends chills up my weak and bettered body. "Walk." The hulk says, his voice serious and mean.

I use all of my energy to slide my feet across the floor toward the door. I feel a shove from behind and I stumble forward catching myself on the door frame. I look out through the door and see long hallways on both sides, as my eyes adjust to the light. Four doors on both sides, then a two-way turn. I hear footsteps walk up behind me. Can I do it? I have to. I have to try to see Kerra again. I take a deep breath and I push off the door frame to the right. I push myself and stumble down the hallway, as I hear footsteps walk into the hallway. "Lest the game begins!" The head honcho yells, and I hear several other cheers throughout the hallways.

Game? Begin? This is what they wanted? Left, or right? Left.

I get to the end of the hallways, and turn left, trying to find somewhere to hide or an exit. Four-way hallway ahead. Left leads me back toward them. I hear laughter followed by footsteps behind me. I look behind me, and see the shadows of the approaching guys behind me. I get to the four-way hallway intersection, and a loud pop behind me makes me turn right.

My legs tremble as I push myself to keep moving. I try all of the doors as I pass them. Locked. Locked. Locked. Let me guess. Locked. I pull myself to the next intersection, my legs trying to give out. My right knee collapses, and I drop to the ground, as I grab a door handle. It turns. I push the door open, and slide in. I slowly and silently close the door. I lean my head back, trying to slow my breathing. I close my eyes, then remember if I could get in, so can they. I reach up, and find the door knob in the darkness. My fingers shake, weakly, as I turn the lock.

I listen quietly to the wall, and I hear a herd of footsteps walk by. The door knob rotates, and the footsteps move on. "We're coming for you!" One of the silent six taunts, as the footsteps walk away.

"Hello?" A soft, young voice whispers, from inside the room with me.

I see a mass standing at the other side of the room. "Are you playing the game?" the young, female voice asks, curiously.

Game? What is this game? "Let me help you." The voice says, making me even more suspicious.

She's probably part of them. You have to get out of here. "You think I'm apart of their team?" The voice says, reading my thoughts.

The lights flash on and start strobbing. I field my eyes, and watch the outline of the female voice walk toward me. I try to get up, but I feel her push me up against the wall. She puts her hand against my throat. "You're right!" she says, with a menacing laugh. "Shall we get started?"

She wraps her arms around me, and pulls me farther into the room. We walk past a white curtain, into a room lit by a single candle in the center. I try to turn around, but she wraps her arm tighter around my neck. "Do you think Kerra would mind if we had a little fun?" She asks, reaching and grabbing my dick and surrounding areas.

I pull away, and she pushes me backwards. I trip and fall to the ground, and try to crawl away from her. How does she know about Kerra? Is Kerra okay? Did they take her?

She launches at me, grabbing my foot. I kick her hand, but her left hand swings a knife into my right shin. I cringe and feel blood dripping down my leg. She leaves the knife in my leg, and pulls me back toward her by my foot. She pulls me farther into the room, toward the candle. I try to fight her off, but my body is too weak to affect her. I kick her hand with my left foot, and she stops. She reached her left hand up my right leg, and pushes the knife in farther. I cringe and gasp slightly, as the pain echoes through my body. She laughs, waving her black and pink pig tails around her head, as she drags me further. We get to the candle and she stops, grabbing it.

"Pretty little candle. Pretty little light. Shining in my hand at night." She sings, turning back toward me. "Oops!" She says, as she tips the hot wax onto me.

I scream as it lands on my bare stomach. "Shh. You don't want the boys to hear you!" She says, kneeling next to me.

She rubs my stomach where the hot wax landed. I tighten my stomach as her chilled fingers, like icicles touch my burned stomach. I slowly crawl away from her. My legs and arms use all the strength they have, to slide me two feet, into a corner. "I love a good chase!" She says, grabbing my foot, pulling me toward her.

I push her back with my foot and she starts laughing, grabbing my ankle and sliding her left hand up my leg. I try to pull my left leg out of her hand, but she quickly drops her weight onto my right leg. I close my eyes in pain as I feel her hand slide up to my pelvis. "Please." I beg, trying to push her off me.

"Please?" She asks. "Well thank you for being polite!"

She reaches over and grabs a metal bottle that was sitting next to me on the floor. She opens the bottle and a rancid smell escapes, making me nauseous. "Acid. A girl's best friend." She says, lifting the bottom of the bottle, slightly above my stomach.

"No. Please! Please! Please!" I beg, trying to get my leg out from underneath her.

I feel tears drip from my eyes. "Please." I beg again, as she lifts the bottom of the half empty bottle further.

"That's right…Beg!" She says with a laugh, topping the bottle so the liquid sits at the edge.

"Please!" I beg, barely able to hear my own voice, as I try to find my way out.

She slides her leg, expecting a splash zone. I use this to kick the bottle toward her. It spills on the front of her. It starts steaming, and she laughs, taking off her shirt. I crawl back into the strobes toward the door.

I get to a cabinet and use it to push myself up. My feet, quickly run toward the door. One slide at the time I make progress, even though my feet are frozen and hurt. She laughs louder as I grab the door handle, remembering I locked it earlier. I turn the lock, my fingers aching, much like the rest of my body. I turn the knob and pull the door open. I am met with a fist to my face by the hulk. I stumble backwards, and to the ground, my head dazed. I try to focus until a large straight object hits me in the back of the head. My head slams forward and the strobes go black, as the female of the game laughs me into unconsciousness.

Chapter 15

Donnie pulls into Kerra's and Ike's driveway. He sees eight police cruisers outside. He quickly gets out, and briskly walks toward the front door. Donnie walks right in, concerned, and is met by the staring faces of nearly a dozen officers. "Where the fuck have you been?" A pissed off female voice that Donnie recognizes as Kerra, asks from the kitchen behind him.

Donnie turns around, meeting Kerra who stops right in front of him. "Well?" She says, her voice filled with anger.

"I went to Henry's last night, wit-"

"Mikeal is missing. And you decide it's a great idea to go and get drunk?" Kerra says, shaking her head in anger and disappointment.

Donnie looks down at the ground, and puts his hands back in his pockets before saying, "I was with Britt."

"I don't care who you were with, you weren't helping us bring him home!" Kerra yells, and all of the officers just stand staring.

"I'm so-"

Donnie stops as the door hits him in the back. He steps forward and Britt slips in. "Sorry Don." Britt says, closing the door.

Donnie looks at Kerra, who rolls her eyes and walks back into the kitchen. Britt looks at Donnie, confused, who fakes a slight smile. "What did I walk into?" Britt asks, and Donnie shakes his head, shrugging, his hands still in his pockets.

Donnie walks into the kitchen where all the police supervisors are. "We need to consider the service truck." Donnie says, turning the corner.

"Why?" Kerra says, rudely.

"Because I think it may help us find him." Donnie says, his eyes locked on Kerra, who is glaring at him.

"What makes you think so?" The police lieutenant, who is sitting at the small kitchen table in front of Donnie, asks.

"It's the only piece that isn't explained." Donnie says, leaning up against the wall, looking at the lieutenant who is on his laptop.

"I checked into it." A young roadie behind Donnie says, stepping forward. "The driver was a mister Jason Wheat of the city maintenance craw."

The rookie hands the lieutenant a manila folder. Inside is the background for Mr. Wheat. "He shared that he had gotten a late-night call for a light out in town, and didn't feel safe to drive home, so he stopped to take a quick nap." The rookie officer continues, as the lieutenant looks through Wheat's file suspiciously. "The last page is the city order for the light to be fixed." The rookie says, lifting the papers up, and pulling out a single piece, handing it to Donnie.

Donnie looks over the document and nods. "He just so happened to pull out moments after the limo crashed right above him?" Donnie says, looking at the picture of Wheats then looking up at the rookie.

"He said he didn't hear anything, and he didn't pull all the way down the road, just enough to where no one would mess with him." The rookie explains, looking between Donnie and his lieutenant, who booth look at him intently. "His boss verified he checked the truck in fifteen minutes after the video shows him leaving the trail below the bridge." The rookie continues as Donnie looks at him, still very suspicious.

"Any other bright ideas, Brainiac?" Kerra asks, still glaring at Donnie in irritation. "Or do you just want to throw your phone again?"

Kerra steps forward and sets a shattered phone onto the table. Donnie looks at the phone, his jaw tight with frustration. "Want to explain that?" Kerra asks, and Donnie can feel there is more to her attitude than him going to Henry's.

"It was an accident." Donnie says, not wanting to tell them about the suspicious phone calls and freezing text messages, until he knows who is sending them.

"An accident that you lost your temper and threw your phone across the room, so hard it shattered?" Kerra asks, coldly, her eyes piercing Donnie with a strong feeling of hate. "Is that the same accident, that you made Ike disappear?"

"Kerra, I-" Donnie pauses, scanning the room. "I didn't- "

"Is that the same accident that sent Zack to the hospital last night?" Kerra asks, catching Donnie off guard, as he didn't know Zack was in the hospital.

"Zack is in the hospital?" Donnie asks, looking at Britt, who is standing behind him. "What happened?"

"Why don't you tell us?" Kerra says, coldly.

"I haven't seen Zack since the hospital after the accident!" Donnie exclaims, as the rookie officer walks up to him.

"Donnie, would you mind coming to the station and answering some questions?" the rooking officer asks, his hands on his gun, and handcuff holder.

"Kerra, are you serious?" Donnie says, confused on why they would think he would hurt his best friend and brother.

"You were the last one alive to see my husband." Kerra says, calmer than she has been.

"Yes, but I would never hurt him! You know that!" Donnie says, nearly in tears with frustration.

"Sir, please come with me." The rookie officer says, grabbing Donnie's arm.

Donnie jerks his arm away from him. "Get off me!" Donnie says, looking at Kerra. "Are you serious?"

"Sir please, just come with me." The rookie grabs Donnie's arm again.

Donnie pulls away and the other rookie officer grabs him, pushing him against the wall. "Donnie, don't fight." Britt says, as the officer's struggle to turn him toward the wall.

A third officer pushes Donnie's face against the wall, while the other two pull his arms together. Donnie feels a pinch as the rookie officer from earlier latches the handcuff on his right wrist. "I swear! I didn't do it!" Donnie says. "Please Kerra, I wouldn't hurt him! He's like a brother to me!"

A tear rolls down Donnie's face, as the officer gets the second cuff on his left wrist. "Please Kerra, don't do this!" Donnie says, looking at Kerra, who doesn't move.

Donnie tries to get out of the officer's grips, but they are all holding him tightly. "Donnie, calm down." Britt says, as the officers pull him away from the wall.

"I didn't do it, Britt!" Donnie says, as the officers push him to walk toward the front door.

"Just stop fighting, we will figure this out." Britt insists, as one of the officers open the door and they walk outside toward one of the rookie's squad car.

Britt follows and watches as the rookie officer leans Donnie against his car. "Do you have anything that can poke me, stick me, or cut me?" The rookie asks, seriously.

"No, but don't check my right ankle, there's not a gun there." Donnie says, sarcastically, looking at Britt, who laughs as the rookie slams Donnie down onto the hood of his squad car.

The rookie grabs Donnie's right ankle, and comes up empty. "I told you, there is not a gun there." Donnie says, his eyes still locked on Britt, who watches with a face of worry.

The rookie lifts Donnie to his feet, and walks him to the back door. The second officer opens the back door, and Donnie gets in without incident, his mind racing about why Kerra would do this to him.

The rookie closes the door and nods at Britt, as he walks to the driver's door on the opposite side of the car. Britt watches the rookie adjust his in-car camera and then drive off. Britt shakes her head and storms back inside. "What the hell was that?" Britt yells, as soon as she breaks the threshold of the door. "Lieutenant, you know he was with me last night and there is no way he hurt Zack."

"Doesn't mean he didn't hurt my husband." Kerra says, coldly, now sitting in the chair adjacent to the police lieutenant.

Britt shakes her head, and replies, "Kerra, he is his best friend, and practically brothers."

"He also has a bad temper that you just saw." Britt's lieutenant says, not looking up from his laptop.

"Why would he hurt Mikeal?" Britt asks, trying to talk common sense into the crowd of her peers, who are blinded by an emotional wife, who just wants her husband home, no matter who it effects.

"I don't know, you will have to ask me!" Kerra says, sternly. "Why don't you ask him, and GET OUT!"

Britt rolls her eyes and shakes her head, walking out of the house. Britt picks up her phone and calls the rookie who took Donnie to the precinct. "Hey, how is he doing?" Britt asks, getting into her car.

"Well, I'm pretty sure, he is going through menopause, because he keeps getting hot and cold flashes." The rookie says, sounding a bit irritated.

Britt laughs, knowing Donnie is driving the rookie nuts. "I'm hot!" Donnie yells, behind the rookie.

"Oh my God!" The rookie exclaims, pissed off.

"Well, I'll let you handle that, and I will meet you at the precinct." Britt says, laughing.

"I'm HOT!" Donnie yells, and the rookie sighs.

"Shut UP!" The rookie says, hanging up the phone.

Britt sets her phone on her passenger seat and drives into town, laughing at Donnie's attempt to annoy the rookie.

Chapter 16

My head. Why does my head hurt so bad? What did she hit me with? Ah, I'm so dizzy. Where am I? My arms, I can't move them. Come on, focus eyes. There are straps around my wrist, that's why I can't move them. My legs are strapped at the ankles too. Not again. I sigh, trying to get out of the straps, knowing it's no used.

"Hey there." The female sadist jumps from behind me. "What are you doing just hanging there?"

"Oh you know, just thinking." I say, sarcastically, my voice low and weak.

"Well, why is your head spinning?" She asks, and quickly pulls the side of the circle I am strapped to.

The circle wheel starts spinning. Round and round. Oh, I'm going to be sick. I close my eyes trying to fight off the dizziness. Good thing I haven't eaten anything in days, or I may be seeing t again soon. Am I slowing down? Please say I'm slowing down. I open my eyes in time to see the female psychopath grab the side of the board, and I come to a halt upside down.

Oh, my stomach. My head is nauseous and my stomach is spinning. "Well, what a convenient stop!" She says, rubbing her hands up my bare legs.

I flinch, and try to get my legs out of her grasp, but the thick, leather like straps are tight and pinch my legs against the hard wood behind me. Her hands stop mid-thigh, and she laughs, before sliding her hands down onto the base of my pelvis. She grabs around my ball sack. I tighten, trying to get her to let go, as she squeezes tighter and tighter. She yanks downward with her other hand, as I cringe in dizziness. I hear her start laughing, and say, "That's for spilling acid on me!"

Tears stream down my face, and my stomach does somersaults, as I start dry heaving from the nausea. She pushes the circle again and it speeds up. I continue dry heaving, my head spinning with nausea, no matter how hard I try to get it to stop. Suddenly I come to a stop right upward, and my head drops as I try to gain my focus. "Well since this is a game, let's play a mini game!" She exclaims, and walks away past the curtain we went through before she hit me in the head with the object. "Oh ladies!" she calls, and suddenly a light shines from behind me.

Several women, some in high heels, walk in, each carrying a weapon. One walks up with a rope and tries to put it around my neck. I move my head, avoiding the noose. One of the other girls, swings a hammer, and hits my knee. I cringe as I hear the hit and caused popping or cracking sound. Pain is sent through my body, and I lean my head forward. The rope lady, the red head, uses this moment to quickly put the double threaded and super thick rope around my neck. I try to shrug it off, but with my arms tightly strapped to the wooden board, it's no use.

The rope girl walks backwards just far enough that my head is pulled forward from the board. I try to pull my head away from her but she yanks my head forward, sending pain through my already pain stricken body. I groan as the lead lady sadist walks up to me,

with a smug look on her face. She reaches up and grabs
the back of my head. Pain is sent through my head, and I
close my eyes, as she pushes her fingertips into what I
can assume is a cut caused by whatever she hit me with.
"this game is simple, we spin you, and try to hit you!"
She says, excited and giddy.

"How is that a game?" I say, still cringing in
pain, her hand still digging into the back of my head.

"Well, okay, it's more of a challenge for
us, and you're our tool." She says, her head twisting into
a creepier, sadistic smile. "Exciting, right?"

She jumps in excitement, and turns toward her
other sadistic girls. "Are we ready?" she asks, shaking
with giddiness and excitement.

"Hell yeah!" The red head says.

"Yeah!" The hammer striker says.

"Let's do this!" the baseball bat or pipe wielding
one yells.

Her partners or lackeys all get excited each
tapping their weapon in their weapon in her hand.
"Alright! Dee you're up first!" The lady honcho shouts,
turning toward me, and spinning the circle. The rope
around my neck tightens, as I start spinning, and the
oxygen is cut off. I see "Dee" who is the one holding the
baseball bat, walk up to me. "Hey batter, batter swing!" I
hear the other girls cheer, as I close my eyes struggling
to breath and fight off the nausea.

I catch a slight movement, right before I feel a
fast hit in my upper thighs. I come back around, and
another hit happen, this time it hits my lower abdomen.
My head gets light headed from the lack of oxygen, even
though it has only been a few seconds. That second hit
knocks the rest of my breath out of my lungs, and I start
to lose consciousness. "Stop!" I hear one of the ladies
yells, as I fight to stay awake.

The spinning stops, and I feel the rope loosen around my neck. I start breathing heavily, trying to catch my breath. "The rope gets too tight." A girl, who is standing right next to me says, and I feel her rubbing the side of my neck.

"Take it off, we will put it back on for part two!" the lady sadist boss says, somewhere across the room from me.

I feel the rope being taken off my neck, as I can slow my heart rate. My body sits frozen with exhaustion and pain. "Unstrap his hands, make it a little more fun for him." The head female honcho says, and I feel two pairs of hands on my wrists.

The pressure is released from my wrists, and I pull my arms into my vision. I rub my sore wrists. "Stru, you're up!" The female boss calls, and I look up at her just in time for her to twist the circle.

My hands drop to my side as my body begins to slide around. Pain shoots through my body, as a blunt object like a ball slams into my stomach. I hear a pop, and another ball slams into my stomach. "Ugh." I hear myself say in echo as I spin fast enough to catch up with my words. Suddenly I get hit with several small blunt objects right after each other in rapid succession. Faster and faster the balls that I watch, are shot out of the baseball pitcher machine the blonde pulled in. The circle slows down, as the balls continue to hit me in the stomach. A hand stops the spin and several groups of balls hit me square in the stomach, as I lay upside down. I cringe, as the same hand starts rotating me to be right side up. As I get to be straight up, my body starts to drop, as the chest strap is released. I have to use the little amount, if any, of energy I have left to hold myself up. "CT, you're up!" the all too happy and peppy sadist says, and the lackey with the hammer walks up, a huge smile on her face.

Again I am spun, this time I struggle to hold onto the straps to keep myself on the board. My head, already nauseous drops toward my chest, making it hard to keep myself on the board. Please let this end! I just want to go home.

CT swings the hammer, and hits me in the thigh, right above the knee. My leg aches, as I focus on not throwing up. I have never done well with spinning rides. Kerra always likes to take me on those pesky tea cup rides, and that never ends well. If the basic spinning isn't enough, she always turns the center piece to make us go even aster. I can't tell you how any times my lunch came back up after those rides. With this game, my past eight lunches want to come right back up, but there's nothing in my stomach to come up. Not even water. My body feels so empty I can nearly feel the blood rushing through my veins and my lungs moving in and out as I breath.

Whack. Oh, God. I hear a crack as CT hits me in my ribs. My lungs shrink into a ball and the low amount of oxygen in my body escapes as I gasp. Tears, that have been dripping from my eyes since the first yank by the honcho lady, come pouring out more. The spinning stops and the girls start laughing. I let my body drop down, as it is completely exhausted and unable to fight anymore. I feel a quick rotation, and I am turned upside down. My hands hang above my head, as I hang there, unable to move. I can feel my oxygen and nutrient empty blood flood my head. I close my heads, trying to find the will to fight more, but I can't find the energy. Kerra, I miss you.

I jump as two cold hands touch my pain stricken thighs. Slide down my thighs and onto my pelvis and stomach. Suddenly I feel hands on my ankles that are above my head. I'm too weak to lift my head to look or fight what they are doing. I just lay there, and suddenly the pressure from the straps is released, and the three sets of hands release their grip on me. Nothing is holding me up anymore, and I quickly learn I cannot fly or hover.

My body, which was restrained about five feet in the car, falls straight down. I try to catch myself, and head a snapping sound, followed by a severe pain, as I land on my already injured right arm. My arm, which contorted under the pressure of my body does not stop my fall, and my head smashes into the solid and cold concrete floor.

As my body fails under the pain of days of torture, I hear maniacal laughing. The laughing morphs into a soothing voice. Kerra? Is that you?

"I'm here Mikeal. Don't give up on me." The soothing voice that I recognize as Kerra says, as warmth washes over my body.

"Don't give up on me." The words echo, as I fall further into the warmth.

Kerra, I love you. I wish we were in New York, or even at our house. The warmth calms my pain and I just lay there, my body finally free from pain. "Don't give up on me." Kerra calls again, and it echoes around my head.

This warmth is so nice, but I have to hold her again. I have to make it up to her. Maybe, take a year off and focus on just her. Relax with her somewhere, maybe Malibu or the mountains away from people. No matter how nice this feels, I have to fight to get back to her. "Don't give up on me" She calls again as the pain starts to flood back into my body and the warmth turns stale and cold.

The light around me begins to face, and turns into darkness. My conscious thoughts fade and for the moment the world disappears into unconscious blackness.

Chapter 17

"What is your date of birth?" The rookie officer asks, annoyed.

"I have my ID in my wallet, if that's easier." Donnie replies, sitting in the chair across from the rookie, still in handcuffs.

"What is your date of birth?" The rookie asks, even more irritated than he was asking the first time.

"March seventeenth of eighty five." Donnie says, quickly.

The rookie types it into his computer, and then stands up. "Come on," The rookie says, and Donnie stands up.

The rookie leads Donnie to the holding cell. Donnie walks in and the rookie closes the door with a loud metal clanking sound. "Let me take the cuffs off." The rookie says, and Donnie walks backwards to the door.

The officer unlocks the handcuffs, and Donnie quickly turns around, and says, "Thanks, Kyle."

Officer Kyle shakes his head, and slams the opening shut, in Donnie's face. Donnie laughs and walks to the bench, sitting down. After only a few minutes of sitting there peacefully, Donnie starts whistling. Officer Kyle looks up, and rolls his eyes, rubbing his fingers through his well gelled hair in annoyance.

After about ten minutes of tuneless whistling Donnie starts whistling the tune of Bad Boys. Officer Kyle looks up from his computer, again, and is at his whit's end with Donnie's shenanigans. "That's enough." Kyle says, and Donnie stops for a moment then starts singing the lyrics.

"Bad boys. Bad boys. What are you gonna do? When they come for you?" Donnie, who knows he is driving the twenty-two-year-old officer nuts, continues to sing as loud as he can.

Donnie stops when he hears a small bang as Officer Kyle throws his pen. Donnie hears a chair slide and hit the wall behind where Officer Kyle is sitting. A loud metallic bang follows, as Officer Kyle swings open the little door opening, that is three times bigger than a mail slot. "Shut up, Donnie!" Officer Kyle says, glaring at Donnie with the hate Kerra looked at him with early.

"Sorry hoss. Don't get your tidy whites in a knot." Donnie says, laughing.

Kyle closes the hatch and resumes his position, typing his report. After a few moments of silence, Donnie starts whistling again, this time to a cartoon theme song. Officer Kyle drops his head onto his laptop, banging it several times in frustration. At this moment, Britt walks in, and Kyle looks at her with rage filled eyes. "Hey Kyle." Britt says, her eyes wide with curiosity to why he looks so pissed off.

Britt looks into the window of the cell and sees Donnie lying on the seat, whistling. "I'm going to kill him." Kyle says, full of burning annoyance. "He will not stop whistling and singing."

Britt laughs, watching Donnie, who looks at the door as she replies, "He's just trying to get under your skin."

"Hey Britt!" Donnie yells, recognizing Britt's voice.

"Hey Don." Britt says, walking over to Kyle, whose face is red, and his fingers are slamming his laptop keys with anger. "What are they charging him with?" Britt asks, looking over Kyle's shoulder.

"Sarg said to do resisting without." Kyle says, looking up at Britt, who is reading his report.

Britt shakes her head. "So basically they made something from nothing?" Britt asks, looking at the wall in front of her, locking eyes with Donnie through the concrete barrier.

"He isn't telling us something." Kyle says, following Britt's glance to the monitor that shows Donnie in the holding cell.

Donnie sits up, looking at the wall knowing, Britt is on the other side. "I know, but this isn't how you will get it out of him." Britt says, still watching the monitor.

Donnie looks down and starts shaking his legs, bored, as he sits in this concrete box, not knowing when they will let him go. "There we go!" Kyle says, as the printer next to him starts printing a document.

Officer Kyle's sergeant walks in. "How long Kyle?" Sergeant Ramos asks.

"Printing now." Kyle says looking toward the printer.

"Cool, Britt, can I talk to you please?" Ramos asks.

"Sure, Sarg." Britt follows Ramos into the hallway. "What's up?"

"I want to take Donnie to an interview room, and I want you to do it." Sergeant Ramos says.

"Why?" Britt asks, hesitating on agreeance to do it, remembering what happened last night.

"He is closer to you, and he will be more willing to talk to you than Kyle or even myself." Sergeant Ramos explains.

"Are we actually arresting him?" Britt asks, not believing that Donnie has anything to do with it.

"Will you do the interview?" Ramos asks, diverting from the question.

"Yes, but he won't give us anything if he is in handcuffs." Britt says, hoping they are going to let him go.

"Okay." Sergeant Ramos says, walking back into the booking room.

Britt follows him, shaking her head. Kyle opens the hatch. "Let's go." Kyle says, and Donnie walks up to the door. "Tur-"

"No handcuffs," Ramos says, looking at Britt who nods.

"Are you sure Sarg?" Kyle asks, worried.

"Yes, no cuffs." Britt says, slightly demanding.

"Ten Four." Kyle says, unlocking the door.

Donnie walks out and sees Britt. "Hey," Donnie says, with a slight smile.

"Hey." Britt says, nodding for Donnie to walk toward the door.

Donnie walks out of the door, followed by the rookie, sergeant, and Britt. Donnie stops in the hallway, allowing the rooking and sergeant to get in front of him, and they lead him through the squad room. "Hey

Donnie!" Officer White, one of Donnie's high school friends, exclaims, walking by.

"Hey Johnny!" Donnie says, turning around to talk to him. "Stay safe out there."

"I will brother!" Officer White says.

"Let's go." Officer Kyle says, pulling Donnie's arm, toward the squad room door.

"Poker when we find Ike?" Donnie asks, ignoring Kyle's pulls.

"Donald!" Kyle says, pulling Donnie backwards.

"Hell yeah, man! Send Kerra my love, I'll be by later to help with the search." Officer White says.

"Sou-"

"Donnie." Britt whispers.

"Sounds good man." Donnie says, finally turning around and walking where Kyle wants him to. "Let's go!" Kyle says, pissed off.

"Sorry." Donnie says, looking at Britt, who is shaking her head, as he winks at her.

Britt shakes her head again, letting a small smile show, as she follows Donnie and Kyle into the interview room lobby that is across the hallway from the squad room. This room is empty, except one table and four chairs. On each of the four walls, there is a single door that leads to the interview rooms. Kyle leads Donnie to the door on the left of the room that has the number one above it. Inside this room is a table along the left wall and two chairs, each in opposing corners of the room. "Sit there, and don't move." Kyle says, pointing to the chair on the opposite side of the room.

Kyle goes to walk out of the room, and stops. "And do me a favor." Kyle pauses, turning back to Donnie. "Don't make a noise until we come back in."

Donnie nods and sits down in the chair. As soon as the interview room door latches, Donnie starts whistling. Kyle stops in his place and closes his eyes in frustration. Sergeant Ramos and Britt laugh, shaking their heads. "Okay, I will start, and if I need you Britt, I will cal-"

The Sergeant's statement is interrupted by Kerra and the lieutenant, walking in. "What is she doing here?" Britt and Kerra ask at the same time.

"We may need both of you." The lieutenant answers, looking between the two women. "We w-"

The lieutenant's statement is interrupted, by Victor and Chris walking into the room, chased by a female records agent. "You can-"

"Where's Donnie?" Victor demands, ignoring the records agent.

"We heard he was arrested." Chris adds on, looking around.

"Sorry Lieutenant Black." The records agent says.

"No problem." Black says, and the records agent leaves. "Sit there and don't move."

Lieutenant Black motions Chris and Victor to sit at the table. They nod and sit down. "Now I'm going to talk to him, Kyle start the recording." Black says, walking into the interview room. "Hello, Mr. Owens." Lieutenant Black says, looking through the folder in his hand.

"Hello, Lieutenant Black." Donnie says, trying to be serious.

Lieutenant Black sits down in the chair across the table from Donnie. "Before we get started talking, I am going to let you know your rights, okay?" Black says, looking up from the folder.

"Yes sir." Donnie says, nodding.

Black reads Donnie his Miranda rights, then sets his folder on the table. "I want to talk to Kyle." Donnie says, winking at the camera, above Lieutenant Black's head.

"Can you tell me what happened after you dropped Zack, Victor, and Chris off at the club?" black asks, ignoring Donnie's request.

"We drove toward Ike's house, and we both got a glass of whiskey. We were joking around when suddenly something or someone hit us." Donnie says, looking directly into his camera, his demeanor completely serious.

"Did something happen between you and Ike?" Lieutenant Black asks.

Donnie looks down from the camera to Lieutenant Black. "Absolutely not. I would never hurt Ike. He is like a brother to me." Donnie explains, looking up at the camera. "If anything, I owe him my life, he saved my life."

"Yes, shows here you have had a rough history. Mostly violent, like far fights, street fights, and aggravated battery with a gun." Lieutenant Black reads from Donnie's criminal history.

"Ike let me be his bodyguard and helped me change." Donnie explains, looking at the ground.

"But you still have a problem with your anger?" Black asks. "Did he make you angry? Did you hit him just a little too hard?"

Donnie looks up, and replies, "No. I didn't touch him!" Donnie's voice is serious and straight forward.

"You didn't argue? Maybe push him and make him hit his head?" Lieutenant Black asks, trying to get Donnie to confess.

"Lieutenant Black, I did not touch Ike. I hit my head in the accident and don't remember anything until I woke up in the hospital." Donnie explains, looking directly into Lieutenant Black's eyes, his mind racing.

"You didn't let your anger slip, one time?" Lieutenant black pushes again.

"No." Donnie says, straight and frustrated at the accusations.

"Not just one time?" Black pushes, trying to get through.

"No. No. No." Donnie says, getting pissed off, his hands shaking, under the table. "I didn't touch or hurt Ike!"

Donnie tries to breath, frustrated. "Then what are you hiding?" Black asks, watching Donnie's hands shake.

"Nothing." Donnie says, biting the side of his mouth.

"What aren't you telling me?" Lieutenant Black asks, pushing hard to get Donnie to confess to doing something to Ike or causing what happened.

"Nothing!" Donnie exclaims. "I'm done. I didn't touch him!"

Black gets up and walks out of the room. Donnie wipes his face, taking a deep breath. Donnie hears yelling out in the interview room. It's Kerra and Britt arguing over who should go into the interview room. "He won't talk to you Kerra, you're the reason he's here." Britt says.

"I'm Ike's wife." Kerra says, determined to get into that room.

"Britt, go." Lieutenant Black says, annoyed.

"Why her?" Kerra says, pissed off.

"She's right, Kerra." Victor says, trying to grab her to calm her down.

Kerra brushes him off, and walks out into the hallway and into the room, where Kyle is watching the interview. Britt walks into the interview room, smiling at Donnie, who is still shaking a bit with the overwhelming anxiety and emotions. Britt walks over to Donnie and hugs him. Donnie starts tearing up in the corner of his eyes, trying to stay strong. "It's okay, Don, just breath." Britt whispers, before sitting down in the chair in front of Donnie.

Donnie looks down, his deep breathing, shaky. "Don, look at me." Britt says softly, and Donnie looks up at her. "They think you're hiding something, and they won't let you go until you tell them/"

"I'm not hiding anything." Donnie says, lowly. "But I think the service truck driver is."

"Okay, let's focus on you." Britt says. "Why did you throw your phone yesterday?"

Donnie hesitates not wanting to talk about, but responds, "Someone kept texting me, the same thing repeatedly. It sent so many times, my phone froze and wouldn't unfreeze."

"Who was it?" Britt asks, curiously, as Donnie hadn't talked to her about any of it.

"I don't know, it was an unknown number." Donnie says. "It had called me previously and gave me a number, but I thought it was my mom, until the number was disconnected when I called."

"Why didn't you tell us sooner?" Britt asks.

Donnie shrugs, knowing he should have at least told Britt. "They didn't give me a chance earlier." Donnie says, looking at the camera. "I didn't hurt Ike, Kerra."

Britt looks up, and Sergeant Ramos walks in. "We'll take him from here Britt. Take Kerra home please."

"What about me?" Donnie asks. "I didn't hurt him. He's my best friend."

Britt gets up and walks out of the interview room. Ramos nods to Donnie to follow her out. Donnie gets up and follows right behind Britt. Donnie stops, and then walks up to Kerra, who is struggling to be mad. He wraps his hands around her, and squeezes tightly. She starts crying and says, "I'm sorry, Donnie."

"Shh. It's okay, baby girl. We will find him and we will bring him home." Donnie says, holding Kerra, who is now sobbing on his chest.

"Come on, let's go home." Donnie says, and Kerra nods, wiping her tears.

A hand grabs Donnie, and pushes him up against a wall. "What are you doing?" Donnie says, trying to turn around.

"Donald Owens, you are under arrest for the disappearance of Mikeal Hemingway." Kyle says, grabbing Donnie's right hand, and putting it quickly in a handcuff.

"I didn't hurt him!" Donnie yells, trying to pull his hands out of the handcuffs.

Victor jumps up, and says, "He didn't touch Ike!"

"Britt, please escort them out of here." Sergeant Ramos says, and Britt looks at Donnie.

"Donnie wouldn't touch him!" Chris says trying to get to Kyle, who double locks Donnie's handcuffs, and pulls him off the wall.

"Vic, Chris, come on." Britt says, locking eyes with Donnie, who is panicking.

"No! He didn't do anything!" Chris says, not wanting to let them take Donnie.

"I know but you can't do anything behind bars." Britt says.

Chris and Victor look at each other, and nod at her common sense. Kyle escorts Donnie, who is completely silent and compliant, out of the room. Britt,

Kerra, Victor, and Chris follow him out, stopping in the hallway, as Kyle leads Donnie out of the building and into the police cruiser. "This is bullshit!" victor exclaims, walking toward the front door of the police department.

The group gets into the parking lot and Kerra says, "Britt, c-"

"No. You know you didn't touch Ike." Britt says, interrupting Kerra.

"How do you know for sure though?" Kerra asks, knowing Donnie didn't touch him, but her emotions is getting the best of her.

"They are best friends, Kerra." Britt says, loudly, "I mean it doesn't take a rocket scientists to see that!"

Britt shakes her head and angrily gets into her car, quickly pulling out of the parking lot. "She's right you know, Kerra?" Victor says, calmly.

"Shut up." Kerra says, getting into the back seat of Victor's car.

Chapter 18

What is that bright light? My eyes are so heavy. That light hurts. I shield my eyes, trying to get my eyes to adjust. My body hurts so bad. I slowly move my head to look around. I am sitting in the hallway, against a hard wall. The bright lights line the hall. Across from me is a door that is very familiar. The sadist lady room is through that door. Why did they let me go?

I hear footsteps in the hallway. "You know, if we catch him, we can gut him." The echoing voice says.

I have to move. I have to go. I move to get up and my arm throbs suddenly, very painfully. My right arm hangs limp, severely bruised and in pain. It is broken, isn't it? I think. I quickly get up, as the footsteps are near. I push myself up with my less pained left arm. My entire body aches. My knees are weak, and give out on me as I try to walk down the hallway. I grab the rail that's on the wall and I drag myself through the hall, tears streaming down my face, as I try to get away from the approaching footsteps.

I take the first turn to the right and slowly drag my body and legs down the hall. My hand slips and I go to fall, reaching out and grabbing a door knob. The knob twists the door opens. My heart drops, as I fall to my knees. I listen to the approaching footsteps, that are maybe halfway down the last hallways I was in. Do I keep going? This maybe another mini game as the head lady called it.

I look down the hall and the closest turn is at the end of the hall. There is no way I will make it before they see me. I take a deep breath, knowing I will regret either decision I make at this moment. I crawl into the room slowly, every muscle and bone in my body sore or broken. I close the door and suddenly, I hear a scream in my ears. I cringe as the blood curdling scream continues. I dig my right ear into my shoulder and cover my left ear with my left hand. The scream still hurts, even though I am shielding my ears.

Something moves in front of me, and suddenly I am in the grasp of a fowl, smelling man in a military like uniform of sorts. "Won't spill what you know?" The man says, as I try to fight him off me, but my body is too weak to even effect or stop him from dragging me where he wants me.

He lifts me off the ground and throws me onto a very hard, and flat surface. I gasp, my breath being knocked out of me. "Last chance!" He yells, loudly, pulling a strap around my stomach.

I can't move, my body is numb with pain. He easily straps my stomach, ankles, and wrists, even though I try to fight him off. "No?" Hey says, grabbing a piece of cloth off the table next to him. "Suit yourself."

He peels the cloth apart and it turns into a bag like the one the head honcho had on my head prior to the "game" starting. My head hurts too much to move, so I try, but he quickly puts the bag over my head. "Stupid terrorist." He says, tightening the bag around my face until it rests pressing firmly against my face, making it hard to breath. "You're going to learn today!"

"I'm. I'm not a terrorist." I say, my mouth masked by the bag to make it come out barely audible. "Please." I beg, my voice raspy and weak.

"Beg all you want, you terrorist, you are gonna learn today!" He says, sternly.

Right after he finishes his sentence, ice cold water starts pouring onto the bag. I cough, the water flooding my eyes, mouth, and nose. My eyes start burning. Salt water. I struggle to breath as the bag constricts more and more. The water stops and I cough, my heart racing uncontrollably. "Ple-"

My begging is cut off by another round of the breath-taking water. The water burns the cuts on my skin. I feel blood in my mouth as the salt dries my already dried lips. I feel my body shaking and with every shake, the pain sears through my body. I get light headed as the lack of oxygen begins to shut down my system. The water stops and again I start coughing, gasping for breath. "Spill and I will take it easy on you." He says, my body in so much pain, I can't reply. "Suit yourself."

The water starts again, this time no salt. I get excited and start taking in as much as I can, even though it is causing me trouble breathing. The military man starts punching me in the stomach, as I try to get as much water as I can through the bag. I gasp with each hit, and start choking on the water. I hear him start laughing as I start fading in and out of consciousness. The water stops and I start coughing, my entire body aches, as I try to stay awake through the pain. I choke as the water drips down my dry throat and freezes on my raw esophagus. The water keeps coming and my body shakes in pain and in attempt to receive oxygen. There is a solid punch to my stomach that sends waves of pain through my body. I clinch my fists and tears instantly fill y eyes as my broken arm throbs with pain.

The water washes my tears away just in time for another punch to my stomach. I gasp, my body unable to move or react. I cough, as the water stops. "Please," I beg, crying.

My tears burn my now salt burnt and frozen cheeks, and I cringe as the guy punches my stomach repeatedly. One hit. Another hit. One after another, and my already weak body can't take it anymore. He laughs, punching me several more times. I feel my body starting to fail and suddenly, I am back in the middle of the warmth.

My eyes wander, my body paralyzed in pain and fear. I try to move, but my body remains limp. The warmth overwhelms my body and finally the pain melts away. I slowly sit up; the memory of the pain still aches through my body. I look around and I see I am in the middle of the bridge. I look to the end and see Kerra standing there. "Don't give up on me, Mikeal." Kerra's voice echoes, as I look toward the other side of the bridge.

I see a gate. An old bronze gate with thick chains and locks across it. On the front of the gate it says, "Closed until a further date."

"Don't give up on me." Kerra's voice echoes again.

The bridge shakes and for a second the warmth dims to coldness. My pain comes back and I collapse into a ball. The warmth comes back and I look at Kerra. "Don't give up on me." She calls, and I pull myself to my feet, using the bridge railing.

I look over the edge and see cold, darkness below. I must make it to her. I turn and start walking toward Kerra. The bridge jerks again, and the pain comes back, sending me to my knees. The warmth strengthens and I get up, nearly running toward Kerra. The bridge shakes again, and I collapse on top of the bridge rail, as the pain shoots through my body. The warmth comes back, but weaker. I can still feel some of the pain, as I walk toward Kerra. Suddenly the bridge gets longer and Kerra is farther away. I speed up trying to get to her, my body aching more and more with each step.

The bridge shakes again, and I collapse to my knees. The warmth fades away completely, as I crawl, trying to get to Kerra. In a blink of an eye, the bridge collapses, and I fall toward the darkness below. "Kerra!" I yell, as I fall farther and farther away from her. After falling for a few seconds, I hit something hard. I cough, my entire body throbbing weakly with pain. I open my eyes, and standing above me is the military dressed man, and he is holding the cloth bag, which drips onto my face. "Hey there terrorist." He says, smiling.

I close my eyes, and feel a tear roll down my cheek, as he raises my head and slips the bag back on. "Please," I ask, muffled by the wet cloth that he tightens around my head.

"Tell me what I want to know, and I'll let you go!" He says.

"I do-"

The water covers my face, this time its burning hot. My muscles tighten, and the pain makes me nauseous. "Don't give up on me." Kerra's voice echoes through my mind, as I struggle to stay awake.

Seconds tick slowly by as if minutes are passing. The water keeps pouring over my pain stricken head. I try to move my head to avoid it, but it follows my head movement. Several punches send pain across my chest. I cough, choking on the burning water. I hear a popping noise followed by creaking, as if a door opened. I choke on the water for a few more seconds, and then it stops. I take rapid breaths and cough, my body aching with every inhale and exhale.

I try to focus on what the guy is doing. I slow my breathing, even though my heart is racing with the need of oxygen. "Did you see the news?" I hear a voice whispers.

"No." The man of water says, in a loud, not so good whisper.

"Wrap this up, and check it out." The voice says.

There is a creak and latching of the door. I close my eyes, knowing the water is coming. I hear footsteps come toward me, followed by pressure on my chest. I cringe, as the pressure gets stronger. My heart races, as the pressure moves around my neck. I try to jerk my head away, as my heart pumps out of my chest. "Don't-"

I fade in and out of consciousness as the lack of oxygen begins to shut my body down again. "Mikeal!" Kerra yells as a bright light shines into my eyes. The pressure is overwhelming, as the lights get brighter. Suddenly the pressure is gone, and the light fades to black.

Chapter 19

Should he be angry? He doesn't know. He understands why Kerra would blame him. He is the last one to see Ike. He tends to have anger issues, but he would never touch Ike. Where is Ike? Is he okay? Did the creepy fan take him?

Donnie's head races with thoughts, as he lays on the hard bed of the jail. It's the middle of the night, but Donnie can't sleep. Is it my fault that he's gone? Did someone take him/? How are things not as they seem? Is it the service truck?

Donnie's thoughts go from blaming himself to the text messages he got to Britt. Tears drip down Donnie's face. He shakes his head in the darkness, frustrated and worried about Ike. Did I hurt Ike? They wouldn't arrest me if they didn't have anything, right?

Donnie starts to doubt what he remembers about that night. The large vehicle hit us, and pushed us through the concrete wall. I sat in the gap. What happened to the other vehicle? Did it leave?

Donnie remembers the lieutenant saying it got towed to the police station. Who was driving it? Was it that truck? The truck driven by the suspicious man who demanded an autograph? What happened?

Donnie rolls onto his right side, toward the wall and tries to fall asleep, his thoughts begging for his attention. He squeezes his eyes shut, trying to fall asleep. The lights start flashing through his shut eyes. As he manages to slip into a light sleep, he gets the feeling he is falling. Metal crushing echoes through his ear drums, as the lights continue to flash. He feels as if he is falling then lands and falls again. He can't see anything but lights, and hear anything but metal crunching, as he falls.

Donnie's heart starts racing as the orange lights start flashing faster by. Donnie stops falling and suddenly there is a loud metal sound. Donnie opens his eyes, and sits up. He sees a deputy in front of his cell, and the cell door opens. His first day in jail for a crime he knows he didn't do starts now.

Kerra walks into the police department, exhausted after searching all night for Ike. Britt is standing by the printer, and she watches Kerra walk toward her. "What do you work every day?" Kerra asks, with a slight smile, trying to be friendly.

"Well, I am officially the lead officer on Ike's disappearance." Britt says, handing the fliers, she just printed to Kerra. "So I will be with you every day."

"So I guess, I'm here to see you?" Kerra asks.

"Indeed, you are!" Britt says. "follow me to the conference room, and I will catch you up on the processing of both vehicles involved in the wreck."

Kerra follows Britt into the conference room, sitting at the table in the center of the room is Victor, Chris, and Zack, who still has a black eye and his right arm is in a cast. "Hey Kerra," Victor says, as they walk into the room.

Kerra looks at Britt, confused about why they are all here. "The driver of the truck was Allan Christopher." Britt explains, opening a folder in front of Kerra. "That night, Allan approached Ike for an autograph several times. The last incident ended with him making an aggressive lung at Ike, and Donnie jumped out of the limo onto him."

"So did you pick him up?" Kerra asks, expecting them to have him in holding.

"He was found dead this morning." Britt says, closing the file. "Cause of death is unknown at this time."

Kerra sits down, tapping her hand on the table in disappointment. "So what's next?" Kerra asks, her face turned with worry about how Mikael.

"We will explore how Christopher was related to Ike's disappearance other than the accident, and follow any leads." Britt says, sitting down next to Kerra. "We are also following the route of the possibility of Donnie hurting Ike."

Kerra nods, her face still stressed. "Do you think Don was involved?" Kerra asks, questioning her and everyone else's accusations of Donnie.

"We don't know for sure, but we are trying to find any leads that will point either way." Britt says, trying to hide her frustration that Kerra sent Donnie to jail.

Kerra nods, as the door flies open, slamming against the wall. Kyle, the rookie who arrested Donnie, quickly walks in. "Britt, we need you." Kyle says, his voice filled with urgency, and stress.

"Stay here." Britt says, jumping up and following Kyle out of the door.

Kyle walks down the hall into the Lieutenant's office. "What's going on?" Britt asks, stopping as she sees Jack Writ, a local news reporter, standing in front of Lieutenant Ramos.

Lieutenant Ramos turns the laptop toward Britt. On the screen are the bolded words, "The Game of Six."

"What is this?" Britt asks, looking between Lieutenant Ramos, Kyle, and Jack, who all have dim and disturbed looks on their faces.

"Close the door, Kyle." Lieutenant Ramos rays, his voice matching the twisted look on his face.

Kyle latches the door and Lieutenant Ramos hits the space bar on the laptop to start the video. Britt's wandering eyes become fixed on the screen, as the words fade away.

Chapter 20

I can't move. My body won't work. The pain is too much. I can hardly even breath. Every movement of the blood in my veins sends pain through my body. Every slow and weak beat of my heart crushes my rib cage. Every cell movement makes my head throb. I open my eyes only to close them again in pain. The bright lights of where I sit burn my darkness dry eyes.

I'm sorry. I feel a light tear as it burns down my cheeks. Kerra, I'm sorry. I can't do it. I pull my knees to my chest, and the pain squeezes my lungs. I let my head fall onto my knees. More pain sears through my weak and beaten body. I ignore the footsteps approaching me, because I don't care if they kill me. As the steps get closer, I start to hear music approaching with them. I know that tune. I know the words. I know that artist. It's me. That's my song. My words. Why are they playing it?

I focus on the music, my body still curled in a ball of pain. The bridge starts, as a hand grabs my shoulder. "You didn't think we would find out who you are, did you?" The voice of the hulk says, as another hand grabs my left shoulder.

"Mister Jeckle, the game is about the get real fun!" A familiar voice says, as I am yanked to my feet.

I feel several pops and pain as I am dragged down the hall. They didn't know who I was? How is that possible? They took me from my limo. "I guess Allan brought us a good one this time." A familiar voice that I can't identify says.

"Too bad, we had to kill him." The hulk says, coldly, followed by a laugh.

My head hangs. My eyes stay shut, as they drag me through the hallways. "Yeah, he was too much of a loose end." The familiar voice says, as we quickly turn a corner.

We stop. I hear a door open then we walk forward. The door shuts and the light that was sneaking through my eyelids disappears. The guys holding me push me forward and I fall onto my knees. I drop toward the ground, catching myself with my left hand. I cough, as pain races through my body. I feel a hand yank my head back, and a bright light sneaks through my eyelids again. The hand holds my head back, as footsteps approach me. "Life is funny. Isn't it?" The voice of the head honcho says. "It's like a game."

I weakly try to pull my head out of the hand grasping it, but the grip gets tighter. My face twists with pain as the hulk pulls my head back, using my matted hair, that is still filled with gel from my hometown concert. "The irony is, we think no one will find our secrets, but they always do." The head honcho says, trying to be prophetic.

I try to open my eyes, but the bright light blinds me. "Isn't that right, Mr. Jeckle?" The head honcho asks, right before someone punches me in the stomach.

Tears drip down my cheeks, as I bring my hands to my stomach. "The iron is, we blame each other when things go bad." The boss says, as another punch hits my stomach. "Much like Kerra is doing to Donnie right now."

Another hit on my stomach, and my knees get weaker than they already were. "You know they arrested him, right?" The head honcho says, as another punch hits my stomach.

I cough, and a liquid comes out of my mouth, landing on my chin. Blood. I taste the unmistakable taste of blood in my mouth. My body sinks, as I continue to cough up blood.

They arrested Donnie? Do they think I'm dead? Why did they arrest him? Why did Kerra let them? My thoughts are interrupted by the brute wall of a man pulling my head upwards. My body raises off the ground, as I feel hands grabbing my wrists. Ropes are tied to my wrists, tightly. My arms are pulled tight out to my sides, as the ropes are yanked in opposite directions.

I feel a pop in both of my shoulders, as they are pulled out of socket. My stomach trembles, as my overworked and under rested nerves pulsate pain signals through my fingers and down into my abdomen. "Please" I beg, my voice hoarse, weak, and barely audible.

I hear a beep, like a button on a phone is pressed. "Hello Mr. Jeckle, welcome to the game!" the head honcho exclaims.

Welcome? Has the game not started? Or is this guy n-

"Round Two!" The crazy, dick master says, and I hear loud clapping around me. "In round 1, you made it through two doors, can you make it through the last four?" The boss says, with what I guess is a sadistic smile on his face to go with his creepy, deep laugh.

I don't think I can make it any longer. My body is too weak. Every organ in my body is bruised, and I think most of my bones are broken. I am at the mercy of what they want to do. Blood drips from the corner of my mouth as the boss says a few more things. I can barely stay conscious, better yet listen to him ramble about this "game".

Wait did he say this room is a door?

"Jep, please do your t-"

His statement is cut short by the distinct sound of a whip cracking. My back contracts in pain, as a quick and sharp hit of a whip cracks against my bare skin. I hear a herd of laughter fill the room, as more quick whips hit my back. Sweat rolls down my forehead, and is chased by tears of pain. My eyes water, and I try to catch the tears with my tongue. Another whip cracks against my back, and I clench my teeth onto my tongue. Blood fills my mouth as my teeth cut deep into my dry tongue.

My head raises with every hit, and drops with a moan of pain. Minutes go by and the whips seem to be harder and faster. My body goes numb. My eyes get heavy, and I want to give up.

"Kerra." I mumble, struggling to breath as the whips crush my ribs into my lungs. "Donnie is innocent." I could hardly hear myself, but I hope she knows this.

I can't get through this. My muscles are too weak to continue. I hear the boss say something, but my body is too busy shutting down to care. I feel my body shake, as I cough. A warm liquid drip out of my mouth, and down onto my stomach. My heart slows, and I feel my head get light.

The whipping stops, and I can breathe again. Slowly I breath in, my rib cage shaking as my lungs expand. The sadist king says something, and I feel a pat on my shoulder.

Focus on what he is saying Ike. Focus!

"The game can only be won, through a battle to the death with me!" The head honcho exclaims. "Don't worry, no one ever makes it that far."

He pats me on the shoulder. I feel several hard taps on my forehead. "Still awake in there?" He asks. "Wakey, Wakey, Bitch!"

A strong punch, sends my head snapping backwards. My head drops immediately, my shoulders and neck, too hurt to hold it up any more. I feel another knock on my head. "Are you awake?" the boss man asks, bending down into my small field of vision with my half-closed eyes.

"Yes" I mumble, the letters hardly making it between my lips.

"Good!" He replies, patting my head.

I would cry right now, but my body no longer has any moisture or liquid in it. "Round two in room three." He says, with a laugh.

The ropes are released and I fall, landing on my knees and hands. My broken arm cries with pain, and it gives out, making me smash my head into the firm concrete floor below me.

If I stay here and don't move, will they leave me alone? A hand grabs me and drags me farther into the room. Well, it was hopeful thinking. The person connected to the hand that is dragging me, stops, and another set of hands help lift me. They drop me hard onto a solid surface. My head is pushed down onto a solid object, and my hands are lifted, and set onto the same object. Another hard object is pushed down around the back of my neck and hands.

I manage to keep my eyes open long enough to see I am locked into some sort of wooden guillotine without the knife. My hands are rested on the wood bottom piece that my neck is locked into. This reminds me of this time Kerra and I went to the renaissance fair.

They had a guillotine, and she dared me to get locked into it. I did, and she made sure it was latched. Then she walked away. She just left me there. No one would help me get out. I asked the guy to help, and he shook his head laughing, as Kerra left me. After she walked away. A big lumberjack, looking guy with a long beard, walked up and asked if I needed help. I said sort of, and he nodded, then turned and walked away. I sat there latched in, and the next thing I knew, the burly man who had walked away just a moment before, came back. This time he was carrying Kerra on his shoulder. He latched her into the guillotine next to me. She was screaming and hollering for him to put her down. I started laughing. When she looked over at me, I saw the spark in her eye, and knew I wanted to be with her for the rest of my life. Something about being locked in a guillotine really helps you figure things out.

Like right now, I have figured out that Round two is going to hurt. How? Well, with a little help from a solid, metal bar, hitting my knuckles. You could say I deducted it. Alternating hits on my hands crush my knuckles against the cedar wood below them.

Cedar? Maybe maple. I don't really know what type of wood it is, all I know is it is really hard. I can feel blood dripping down my fingers, as the hits continue. Drip, drip, whack. Drip whack. Drip, drip, drip. There is an extended pause between hits. I take a deep breath, preparing for another hit.

What happened next, I didn't see coming. The blinding light that follows me from round one turns off. I hear a metal object hit the floor. After a few seconds, I hear the distinct sound of a large group of people walking away from me. The steps get fainter, and I hear the creaking of a door opening. I hear the footsteps continue walking out of the room. One at a time the footsteps fade away, until the last one walks out. I hear the creaking of the door, and a light sound of it latching. Then all I hear is silence.

Before, I thought silence was terrible, but now it means an absence of hits and chokes, and cringes of pain. An absence of the pain causing people. The absences of having to struggle to live, more than I already am with my exhausted body. It is also the presence of rest.

Chapter 21

Donnie is brought to the jail cafeteria, where he is served oatmeal by other inmates. After getting his food, Donnie finds a seat away from everyone. Still fighting his tiredness, due to lack of sleep, Donnie slowly eats his breakfast, even though he hates oatmeal. A bigger guy, who looks like he could swallow Donnie whole, sits down in front of him.

Donnie who is spinning his plastic spoon around his half-eaten oatmeal, glances up at the guy quickly. "You're Jeckle's friend." The guy says, catching Donnie's attention.

Donnie nods slightly. "Why are you here?" The guy asks, pressing into Donnie, as if he already knows.

Donnie, who really isn't in the mood to talk, shrugs his shoulders. "Cause he killed Jeckle." Another guy, with bright reddish orange hair says, sitting down next to the first big guy.

"Say what?" The brown- haired guy, who was first to sit down, exclaims.

Donnie keeps his head toward his plate, knowing he didn't kill anyone. {"Yeah they said the accident was a way to hide it." The scrawnier, but still muscular guy says, trying to egg on a fight.

Donnie ignores them, still spinning his spoon on his plate. "Well damn man, I am a huge Jeckle fan." The big guy says, now pissed off at Donnie.

"He's not dead." Donnie mumbles, not looking away from his plate.

"Where is he then?" The big guy replies, leaning in closer to Donnie. "What did you do to him?

"Nothing. I didn't touch him." Donnie says, annoyed, still not looking up from his food, even though he lost his appetite when the guy sat down.

"You probably got rid of him because you were jealous!" The scrawny guy says, trying to get the big guy to fight Donnie.

Donnie shakes his head, holding back the frustration and emotions of guilt, as he gets up and walks straight toward the door. The big guy grabs Donnie's arm and pushes him against the wall. The scrawny guy gets up and jumps excited, as the big guy, pulls Donnie over the table to the same side as him by the front of his shirt. Donnie tries to slip out of the guy's grip, but the guy slams him against the wall. "Where is he man?" The big guy says, his voice deep and stern.

"Get off of me." Donnie says emotionless, about to snap this guy's arm.

A guard walks up, and says, "Do we have a problem?"

"No sir." The big guy says, and leans into Donnie. "You better tell them where he is, or you're a dead man."

The man let's go of Donnie, who pushes him back. Donnie's push doesn't affect the guy, as he walks straight toward the door. "Hey guys, that guy touched a kid!" The scrawny guy yells, not happy that his friend didn't beat Donnie into the hospital.

Donnie shakes his head, and looks straight at the door, which quickly opens, displaying Britt, who smiles slightly. "Pervert!" A bunch of guys yell, as few standing up, and trying to come after Donnie.

Donnie puts his hands up, and the door guard pats him down. The guard nods, and Donnie walks straight toward Britt. "Please tell me, you bring good news?" Donnie says, getting through one door and walking to the second, where Britt is standing.

Britt tosses Donnie his leather jacket that he left at her house. Donnie catches it, and stops. "As much as I love the color orange on you, I prefer your leather." Britt says, winking.

Donnie looks at her, slightly confused, but with a smile. "Let's go home, cowboy." Britt says, and Donnie smiles bigger, looking behind him as the guys stand at the first door he went through.

Donnie nods, and follows Britt out of the jail. "How did yo-"

"I didn't, the evidence did." Britt says, as they walk toward Britt's car.

As they get closer, Donnie sees Kerra standing in front of Britt's car, tears rolling down her cheeks. They approach, and Kerra walks up to Donnie, who is now wearing basketball shorts and a white t-shirt that Britt brought him. Kerra wraps her arms around him, and starts sobbing. "I'm so sorry." Kerra says, through the flood of tears.

Donnie tears up, and holds her tight against his chest. He doesn't say anything, but Kerra calms down, as he holds her, knowing that while deep down he is frustrated, he isn't mad at her. Donnie lays his chin on the top of her head, and they stand there for several long minutes, both overwhelmed with the emotional occurrences of the past three weeks. Donnie looks over at Britt, who smiles, admiring the sweet moment. "You want in on this?" Donnie asks, letting go of Kerra and running at Britt.

Donnie wraps Britt in a bear hug, and Kerra laughs, as Britt exclaims, "Oh, my goodness! Donnie!"

They all laugh and Donnie releases Britt from the hug. "Didn't want you to feel left out of a sappy moment." Donnie says, looking at Britt, whose face is red with laughter.

"Well thank you." Britt says, winking.

Donnie wraps his arms around the shoulders of Britt and Kerra. "Where ever we are heading, I need some food!" Donnie says. "Four days in jail, and I am starving."

"We can make that happen!" Kerra says, as they walk toward Britt's Dodge Challenger.

Donnie quickly grabs the passenger door handle and swings the door open, motioning for Kerra to get in. Kerra gets into the front passenger seat, and Donnie gently closes the door. Donnie gets into the back seat and slides to the center seat. Donnie leans forward as Britt turns on the car. "Where are we heading?" Donnie asks, looking between Britt and Kerra.

"To see your best buddy, Kyle!" Kerra says, sarcastically as Britt turns the car around and pulls away from the jail.

"So perv, what do you want to eat?" Britt asks, teasing Donnie.

"I was thinking, little children." Donnie shoots back.

Britt and Donnie bust out laughing, and Donnie leans his head back. Kerra looks at them with a concerned and confused look, as Donnie's face turns bright red. "What the hell?" Kerra asks, starting to laugh at them.

Donnie wipes his eyes, taking a deep breath, before replying, "Funny jail people." Donnie shakes his head, with another chuckle.

Kerra shakes her head, rolling her eyes, with a smile lightening her stressed face. Donnie takes another deep breath and leans back forward. "So what are those food options?" Donnie asks, looking out the front windshield.

"We got all the fast food you want!" Britt says, with sassy head shake.

"I don't care, but a big cheeseburger sounds super good." Donnie says, nodding. "So first food place you see!"

Kerra nods in agreeance, as Britt turns the car onto the main highway of their hometown. Donnie looks over, as they pull past the arena Ike performed at the night he went missing. The large sign celebrating Ike's performance is still hanging on the chain link fence in front of the arena. Britt reaches back and sets her hand gently on Donnie's leg, trying to comfort him, his face now tense. Britt comes to a red light and eases into the left turn lane to go toward the town center. "So, you said evidence. Do they have any leads?" Donnie asks, his mind back to dwelling on Ike.

"We do, that is why we are going to see Kyle." Britt says, locking eyes quickly with Kerra, sharing the same thought as her.

Donnie nods, as they pull into a fast food restaurant. Donnie reaches into the internal pocked in his leather jacket and pulls out his trifold wallet that Britt put in there before they left the jail. "I got it Don." Kerra says, looking through the rear view mirror.

Donnie looks up and nods, slipping his wallet into his pocket. Britt orders the food, and Kerra hands Donnie his, as the car pulls toward the police department which is about two miles from them. Donnie opens his burger and takes a bit, his taste buds salivating as it melts in his mouth. Kerra watches Donnie through the rear view mirror, and laughs as they stop at a stoplight.

Kerra's head is filled with guilt and self-blame, and she watches him. Why did I suspect Don? I should have been at the concert. I shouldn't have said I was tired. Would he still be here if I had? Kerra thinks all of these thoughts, as she watches Donnie slowly devour the double cheeseburger in his hands. The car behind Britt honks, and Kerra looks up, realizing she had zoned out.

Donnie, who had been watching Kerra through his peripheral, leans forward. Donnie thinks about what to say, but leans back, unable to find the words. Britt pulls into the police department, and Donnie continues to rack his brain to think of what to tell Kerra.

Britt parks the car, and all three of them get out, carrying their bags of food. Donnie has an epiphany, as he looks at the department building, and says, "Hey Kerra."

Kerra, who is in front of Donnie looks back, and then turns around. Donnie catches up, and Kerra says, "What's up?"

Donnie wraps his arms around Kerra and says, "I can't make your pain go away. I can't tell you where Ike is, but I can tell you that through whatever happens and has happened, I love you, and I will always be here for you and Ike."

Kerra hugs Donnie back, tears streaming down her face. Britt watches, getting tears in her eyes at the same time. Donnie tries to stay strong, allowing only one tear to roll down his cheek. The front doors of the police department swing open, and Kyle busts through stopping the door with his foot. "Britt, we have a break!" Kyle says, yelling with urgency.

Kerra looks at Britt, who walks toward Kyle. Donnie and Kerra run to keep up with Britt as they all follow Kyle into the department. "An anonymous caller called and identified a man from the video." Kyle says, as they all walk quickly through the police department.

Donnie looks at all three of them, confused. "What video?" Donnie asks, as they turn the corner down the hallway that leads to Lieutenant Ramos's office.

"They sent us a video." Britt explains. "Well Jack Writ of the local news channel.

"Who's they?" Donnie asks, confused as why this is the first time he has heard about it.

Donnie, who had been eating fries, drops the half full container in the trash can, as they pass, his appetite completely gone. "We are trying to figure that out." Kyle says, walking into Ramos's office.

Kerra follows, and Britt stops in the door way, turning toward Donnie. "What are you doing?" Donnie says, his heart pumping with frustration and anxiety now.

"I need you to just breath. We will only show you this video if you can stay calm." Britt says seriously, making Donnie even more anxious.

"Okay." Donnie says, nodding, his right hand shaking, as his heart continues to race.

Britt turns and walks in. Donnie follows, trying to calm down. "Hey Donnie." Ramos says, a laptop in front of him. "Sit down for me please."

Lieutenant Ramos points to the seat in front of him. "I'm go-" Donnie pauses, seeing Britt's disapproving eyes looking at him. "Okay."

Donnie turns the seat around, and straddles it, leaning his chin on the back of the chair. Kerra, who has seen the video, slips out into the hallway, before Kyle closes the door. Kyle latches the door, and Donnie glances back, quickly, his attention diverted back to Lieutenant Ramos as he rotates the laptop that is sitting in front of him toward Donnie. Without hesitation, Ramos hits the space button and the black screen turns into the words, "The Game of Six".

The video starts to play, and Donnie's eyes are locked on the screen. He hears a man talking about irony, but his eyes are focused on the battered, naked body of the man tied up. He knows who he is. Donnie's stomach churns with anger and desperation as the video continues. He cringes as a whip strikes the familiar man's back. He hears his name mentioned, but his focus is on the cut, skinny, and bruised body that is strung by ropes behind the man talking. Tears start streaming down Donnie's face, but he doesn't move, his body tense as the man is released and sent to the ground. The man is carried to a new position by two muscular men, and locked in some sort of wooden head lock.

Britt walks up to Donnie, putting her hands on his shoulders. Donnie doesn't move, as he watches the man get hit on his hands are hit with a bar, as they are locked in the same wooden box as his head. The video ends, and Donnie just sits there, staring at the blank black screen in front of him. Britt squeezes his shoulders, but Donnie just sits there paralyzed. Finally, he manages to say, "I'm going to kill, each and every one of them."

Donnie's words are drawn out by a pause in between each one. Tears continue to pour down Donnie's cheeks, as Lieutenant Ramos nods and Britt, who is in uniform, bends down and wraps her arms around the front of Donnie, who is turned away from her. Donnie continues to stare at the now black, computer screen, his heart racing, and fists tightened with anger.

Donnie wants to run out of here and find these people. He wants to scream. His anger is boiling, but he told Britt he would stay calm. Donnie's fists start

shaking, as he tries to calm himself down. Britt squeezes
him tighter, as more tears drip from his eyes. Lieutenant
Ramos watches Donnie, whose eyes are locked on the
screen. Donnie reaches to start the video again, but Britt
and Ramos grab his hand. "I have to figure out who they
are." Donnie says, his voice trembling with emotion.

"We will figure it out, you don't need to watch
that again." Britt says, as she feels Donnie trembling in
her arms.

"Do we-" Donnie pauses, wiping his face. "Do
we know who any of these guys are?"

"We know who two are." Kyle says, from
behind Donnie.

Donnie turns around, and Britt moves out the
way to expose Kyle who is standing against the side wall
of the room. "Do we know where these two are?"
Donnie asks, his hands still trembling, but his heart rate
slowing down.

"One is dead at the morgue, and the other is in
interview room 1." Kyle says, giving a sense of hope to
Donnie, who nods, shaking.

"Why are we sitting here then?" Donnie asks,
standing up.

Donnie walks out of the room, followed by Britt
and Kyle. The reporter waits as Lieutenant Ramos stands
up. "After you." Ramos says, motioning for the reporter
to walk in front of him.

They all walk into the conference room of the
police department, where the cameras for the interview
room are displayed on the television. Every one sits
down, and Lieutenant Ramos nods at Kyle who walks
out of the room. Britt grabs Donnie's left hand sliding
her chair next to his, and away from the table. Donnie
looks at her and smiles a pain filled smile. Lieutenant
Ramos turns up the television, as Kyle walks into the
interview room. "Hello Mr. Drake, I am officer Kyle,"

Kyle says, sitting across from a brown-haired guy, who is looking smugly at the camera. "DO you know why you are here today?"

The guy doesn't answer, he just looks at the camera, a half-lifted smile on his face. "Mr. Drake?" Kyle asks, following his glance to the camera.

"The game is just starting. He is the only one who can stop it." Mr. Drake says, followed by a menacing laugh.

Donnie leans forward, looking deep into the screen, as if he was staring directly into the eyes of Mr. Drake. "I have a message for Donnie from Ike." Mr. Drake says, his eyes still piercing into the camera.

Donnie stands up and walks up to the screen, his heart beginning to race again. "Frites." Drake says, with a laugh.

"Fries?" Britt says, walking to Donnie who stands there stiff.

"Did you really think Ike was chosen at random?" Mr. Drake says, his eyes locked with Donnie's through the camera. "We've been watching you. Did you tell his wife the secret yet?"

Donnie just stands there, all eyes turn from the screen to him, as Mr. Drake begins laughing. "Mr. Drake, I have-"

"I'd like to talk to my lawyer." Mr. Drake says, interrupting Kyle, as he glances into the camera.

Kyle gets up and walks out of the interview room and Donnie watches as a uniformed officer walk in after him. The officer walks Mr. Drake out, as Kyle walks into the conference room closing the door firmly. He sits down in the chair behind Donnie. "So, Donnie, got anything you want to tell us?" Kyle asks, laying his chin on his hands irritated.

Donnie stands staring at the now empty interview room, his mind racing with memories. "Donnie?" Kyle says, trying to usher Donnie on.

Donnie stands there, frozen, his mind filled with rage. His legs are numb. His heart is throbbing as if it's going to fall out of his chest. "Donnie?" Britt asks, concerned.

Donnie's hands shake, as he tries to calm down. Britt grabs Donnie's arm, and he quickly pulls his arm away. He turns, his face bright red, as if sunburned. Donnie walks out of the room. Everyone looks at each other, as Britt follows him out.

Donnie makes it outside, and keels over in the grass right outside the front door. He throws up, as Britt walks outside. Britt quickly puts her hand on his shoulder, and he pushes it off, quickly standing up and walking away from her. "Donnie." Britt says, as Donnie walks toward the exit of the parking lot.

Donnie ignores her, and she runs after him. She grabs his arm, and he pushes her off, and turns around. "Just let me be." Donnie says, irritated and stern.

"You don't have to do this by yourself." Britt says, stopping on the edge of the parking lot. Donnie doesn't answer, but sticks his hands in the pockets of his basketball shorts, as he walks across the street. As he walks, his mind drifts away from the present, and begins flashing scenes from past moments with Ike.

Donnie and Ike are sitting in a small, dimly lit diner. Their booth is sitting in the middle of the rectangle room, along the left wall. Other booths line the wall in front and behind them, but only a few of them have people in them. "She has no idea?" Donnie asks sitting across a table from Ike.

"Not a hint! I want to spoil her." Ike says, excited, smiling nonstop.

"How are you going to communicate there?" Donnie asks, taking a sip of beer.

"They speak English over there." Ike says, slightly getting worried.

"What if someone doesn't?" Donnie asks. "Like how do you say fries?"

Donnie puts a couple of fries into his mouth, leaning back in his seat, waiting on Ike's response.

"French de fries?" Ike says, laughing.

Donnie and Ike laugh, both eating fries. "Sounds right to me." Donnie says, both still laughing.

After they calm down, Ike asks, "So whats the right answer?"

"I have no clue." Donnie says, with a slight chuckle, taking a sip of his half full beer.

"Frites," an old man says, behind Donnie. Donnie looks back at him, caught off guard by the man's response, and says, "What?"

"Frites." An old man repeats, leaning back to his table.

Donnie and Ike start laughing to themselves. "You got this man." Donnie says, through his quiet laugh.

"I hope so, just want to try to make up for lost time, you know?" Ike says, taking a sip of his beer, that he has barely touched.

"Damn dude, like can I be your wife?" Donnie says, laughing. "You guys travel the world together, and you still spoil her!"

Ike laughs, and shrugs. "We already spend just as much time together than I do with her." Ike says. "We might as well be a love triangle."

Ike and Donnie laugh, as the waitress comes up. "Can I get you another beer?" she asks, as Donnie drinks the last gulp of his beer.

"Yeah, bring another round for both of us please." Donnie says, looking at Ike's quarter empty beer.

The blonde waitress nods, and says, "I'll be right back!"
The fit waitress, turns and walks away, Donnie's eyes checking her butt out as she walks toward the bar area across the room. Ike leans in, and says, "So man, when are you going to settle down?"

Donnie's eyes get big and he laughs slightly, while replying, "When I can find a girl who can handle me."

"Yeah, you know what?" Ike pauses. "You might find better luck with getting a dog."

"That's why I got you." Donnie says, then barks. "Dogs are easier, because they don't talk back."

Both Ike and Donnie laugh. "They also can't satisfy all of your human needs." The gray-haired man, behind Donnie says, eavesdropping on their conversation.

Donnie looks back, slightly shocked, his eyes locking with Ike, when he looks back forward. Ike tries to hold in his laughter, as Donnie responds, "Yeah, but my right hand can satisfy them just fine."

Ike busts out laughing, as the man turns toward them, his graying beard catches the light as is dark eyes stare at Ike, who quickly shuts up. "You boys will learn, life is a game. You can't just be there when you want to be or can. You'll lose if you don't fall in line with those around you." The man says, turning back around.

"Fuck lines. I prefer curves." Donnie says, grabbing the beer the waitress sets down in front of him, as he quickly glances down her side with his eyes. "Cheers to curves and fun."

Donnie and Ike cheers, brushing off the words of the eavesdropping man behind them. The man gets up, and walks out of the diner. "Who was that?" Ike asks the waitress, who is still standing there, shocked at the seriousness of the man's attitude.

"I've never seen him before." She says, with a laugh.

"He's a fucking loser." Donnie says, laughing as he takes a drink of his beer. "But at least he got one part right."

Ike and the waitress look at Donnie curious as to what he thinks the guy got correct. "Life is a game. One where we all die, so I guess we all lose in the end."

Donnie finishes his beer, shaking his head. "It's the journey, not the destination." The waitress says, rubbing Donnie's shoulder as she walks away.

Donnie turns his head back, checking the out the waitress again as she walks to another table. "Damn. He says, his eyes watching her hips shake as she walks out of the dining area and into the kitchen.

Ike barks, and Donnie laughs, sitting back in his seat.

Chapter 22

Sitting in the darkness for a long time can make a person crazy. Sitting in the darkness, unable to move because of pain. Every noise echoes and every heart beat repeats forever. You try to sleep, but you are afraid if you do, you won't wake up. Afraid they will come back and you'll wake up in more pain. Afraid you won't see your wife again. Afraid this darkness is the last thing you will see.

Here I sit. My arms, legs, and head strapped, as I knee on the ground. My knees ache as does every other part of my body. I try to rotate my wrists to release pressure, but it sends a wave of pain through my body. My body cringes, sending more pain down my spine. I would cry, but I am so dehydrated, no tears will fall. I want to yell out but my throat feels as though it is full of sand that grinds every time I breathe in. The only thing I can think of is seeing Kerra and holding her in my arms.

My heart drops, as I hear a crashing sound, as if a door was slammed open. My heart starts racing as I hear footsteps approach me in the darkness. I close my eyes, expecting pain, as the footsteps stop next to me. A hand grabs my chin, and turns it to the left. "Welcome to level three." A deep male voice says, as I feel my body tremble.

I don't know if I can survive any more rounds. I don't know if I can even survive another hit. My body is ready to give up. My body is ready for rest. Eternal rest does sound peaceful right now.

I feel the pressure around my head and arms lessen, as a loud bang occurs as an object drops in front of me. I jump, stumbling backwards, my ankles still strapped. Pain surges through my body, like an earthquake through a city. I land on my heels, and fall back forward onto my arms in pain.

The pressure on my ankles disappears, but I lay there frozen in pain. "Begin." The deep male voice from before says.

I lay there, too weak to move, too afraid to talk. AS I expected, I am ripped from the ground by my matted and blood filled hair. I cringe as my body leaves the ground. I land hard on the ground, after my back meets the hard surface of a wall. All the air, well the little there was, leaves my lungs. I try to get up, but I can't even get my chest to move, no matter how hard I try. A hand grabs the back of my next and lifts me off the ground. My head is slammed into a wall several times. My little bit of consciousness starts to slip away as I hear the male from a few minutes ago, say, "Okay, Hulk, stop playing, and strap him up, so our new clients can have some fun."

Clients? More sadistic assholes? AS if the ones here weren't enough to kill me. I feel the person holding me walk across the room. My body still suspended in the air, as they carry me. I am slammed against a hard surface, as four other hands strap my arms and legs down. I open my eyes, but the huge hand of Hulk blocks me from seeing anything.

The four hands latching my body parts down, let go, and after a few seconds Hulk lets go of my face. A heavy pair of footsteps walk away, as a softer pair walk toward me. "Welcome to the game of six. Conform and live. Disobey and get punished." A male voice, belonging to the head honcho, I think, says, patting me on my back.

I shiver, my body trembling in fear and gut wrenching pain. "For now on, your name is David, understand?" The man's voice turns harsh.

I try to nod, but I am frozen. "I said, do you understand?" the man says, as a hand presses firmly onto my back.

The hand presses harder and harder, sending the pain, from my broken ribs, rushing through my body like a thousand bulls in a stampede. To get the pain to stop, I use all of my energy to nod, and say, "yes," very lowly and weak.

"Good." the man's voice says, as the hand releases my back. "So David, this game is easy. You do what we say, and all is good."

My body trembles in fear, as the man explains the game, again. Have I not been in the game this entire time? Game of Six? What does that mean?

"However, there is an added part. If the viewers don't do what we say, you'll also get punished!"

"Too easy." A female voice, says.

I recognize these voices, but my eyes won't focus to identify the face of each one. The female voice is the all too familiar sadist with the "girl" room.

Several females laugh, as a sudden whip of something sharp hits my back and my weak body cringes in pain, as the tensing of my back seizes in a severe cramp. "Oops my bad." the falsely sweet female voice says, as tears stream down my face, as I try to get my back to relax again.

"First order of business, David, you need to beg for your life." The head honcho says.

My body is so weak. My lips dry. My eyes nearly swollen shut and unable to focus on anything. "Beg!" The boss man demands, as a sharp object whips my back.

I try to mutter the word please, but nothing comes out. "Beg!" The king sadist yells, and I am whipped again.

Tears that are already pouring from my eyes, drip faster, stringing my injured face. "Pl-"

"Beg!" He yells again, and several swift whips hit my back.

I try to beg, but nothing will come out. All my body will do is lay here, frozen, as it shakes after each hit. "You're not off to a good start." The head honcho says, as a first object pressure onto my back.

I cringe, my body going numb. The pressure continues as several whips hit my lower and upper back. I gasp for breathe, my body overwhelmed. "Please" I mutter unable to move or say more.

"What was that?" The head boss man says, as the pressure releases.

"Please." I mutter trying to get breath.

"Close." The boss man says, as the whip hits my lower neck right in between my shoulder blades.

"Please." I pauses, gasping for a low amount of breath to fill my lungs. "Please!" I beg, my body pushing all my air out with the syllables.

"Much better." The head honcho says, and another whip hits my back.

"Oops!" The female sadist voice says, laughing innocently.

I try to calm my body down, but it gets worse, as two hands slide down my back. "You live, you love, you laugh, and you cry." A female voice says, her hands rubbing down my bare, bleeding back. "You learn, you grow, you fall, you hurt."

"Life is about learning and growing, but pain is part of that, and through it all you will lose if you don't fall in line." The head honcho says, trying to sound prophetic.

"You life, you love, you laugh, you cry." The female repeats, as she slaps my back, sending shocks of pain surging through my bones.

"This one is for the audience. Pain is apart of life, and while David is in pain, so should his best friend."

"You learn, you grow, you fall, you hurt." The female sadist says, dragging her sharp nails down my cut back.

"His name is Donnie. He was in jail for the crime, but he has been released. Find him, and bring him pain." The head honcho explains, and I try to get out of the straps that are connected to my arms and legs. "If you can complete this task, David shall be spared. You all have twenty-four hours." The head honcho demands, as the female sadists sticks her finger in one of the most painful cuts on my back.

"Please" I beg, now worried about Donnie's safety. "Don't hurt him."

"Oh we aren't going to silly, they are!" The female sadist says, patting me aggressively on my back.

"Check the comments for all the information you need on the target." The head honcho says. "We will kick David's ass until then."

The main female giggles, and I feel a sharp whipping pain on my back. The pain continues as the whipping gets quicker and quicker. "Hand me the bat." The boss lady says, I'm guessing addressing her partners.

I prepare, knowing pain is coming. My body shakes so bad, I can't keep my eyes open because of the pain. A firm and strong strike of a solid object, like a baseball bat, hits the middle of my back. All of my breath leaves my body. Trying to stay conscious, I gasp, trying to find fresh air through the pain. Hit after hit. Breathtaking blow after energy draining hit. My eyes, already weak and heavy, try to stay open, but get weaker and weaker. I try to breath in between the hits, but my lungs lock, aching in pain. I gasp as a sixth blow hits my back. Due to lack of consciousness, my head begins to droop toward the ground. My already spinning head, races in circles, as I fade from consciousness.

Chapter 23

A soft breeze travels through the silent trees, as Donnie sits on the picnic bench near the red clay falls. "The memories are like the mind's way to drive you insane." Donnie says, knowing Britt is walking up behind him.

"Memories also serve as a way to solve questions of the future." Britt says, stopping beside Donnie.

"How do they answer questions, yet give you more?" Donnie asks, looking out across the wide plains of trees that stretch far beyond the horizon.

"Memories are like a scavenger hunt, you follow and find one thing then you get a clue to the next place you have to go." Britt depicts, sliding onto the picnic bench next to Donnie.

Britt's phone starts to ring, but she ignores it, gazing out across the same plains as Donnie. "Memories are like nature,k you can't predict what's in them, but you can make a pretty good guess." Britt says, putting her hand on Donnie's leg, as the sun gets close to setting

behind the hills. "I know you remember something."
Britt says, looking at Donnie.

"Just a face. No names. No way to know who he
is." Donnie says, not taking his eyes off of the trees.

Donnie hands Britt a notebook, that is opened to
a well organized list. "Mid-forties, brown hair, and
heavier set." Britt reads, going through the list. "Do you
know where to find him?"

"I don't even know who HE is! Or who the guy
was with him is." Donnie says. "But I-"

Britt's phone goes off again. Britt ignores it.
"You?" Britt asks, as Donnie's eyes go narrow.

"I know how to find out." Donnie says,
jumping up and heading to his truck.

Britt's phone rings again and she answers it, as
Donnie gets into his truck and quickly backs out.

"Britt," she says.

"Where's Donnie?" Officer White asks,
his voice filled with concern.

"He just pulled out, I'm following him." Britt
says, getting into her Charger, pulling out, trying to
catch up with Donnie.

"You need to get him here…" White says. "Like
now" Concern fills his voice, making Britt a bit
suspicious.

"Why?" Britt asks, speeding up behind Donnie.

"Just get here, as soon as you can." White says,
hanging up abruptly.

Britt honks trying to get Donnie's
attention. Donnie keeps driving, his mind determined to
get to its destination. Britt pulls beside Donnie, honking.
Donnie looks over and Britt waves for him to pull over,
knowing he doesn't have his phone with him. Donnie
looks curious at her shrugging, not wanting to stop,
because his mind is set on where he needs to go. Britt
urgently waves for him to pull over, her face serious.

Donnie rolls his eyes, and pulls over into the parking of a local gas station. Britt puts her car in park and runs up to Donnie's window. "White needs us at the department." Britt says.

"For what?" Donnie asks, annoyed.

"I don't know but it sounds urgent." Britt says.

"Well, unless they found Ike, he can wait." Donnie says, putting his truck in gear and driving out of the parking lot.

"Okay.. Then." Britt says, turning and getting into her car.

By the time Britt turns out onto the road, Donnie is nowhere to be found. "Really, Donnie?" Britt mumbles, shaking her head, as she drives down the road looking down each side road, trying to find him.

Britt doesn't see Donnie's truck at all, as she drives nearly five miles down the road. She pulls over, trying to decide what to do.

Donnie drives toward the outskirts of town, his left hand tapping the steering wheel with anxiousness. Donnie pulls into a driveway of an older brick house with a leaf covered yard. Donnie gets out of his truck, fidgeting with his keys.

As Donnie walks toward the front door, he sees two guys walking across the street looking at him. Donnie gets to the front door and slips his key into lock, turning the knob, and walking inside, as the two guys step onto the concrete, closely watching Donnie.

Donnie, on a mission, walks straight to the back bedroom, and grabs a laptop off the nightstand next to the bed. He drops it on the bed, and bends down, onto his knee, looking through the files. "Where are you?" Donnie mumbles, flipping form file to file, looking for something that will give him a lead. "Oh, I know!" Donnie says, pulling up an internet browser.

Donnie goes to the Mr. Jeckle website, and clicks on the gallery link. "Colorado." Donnie whispers to himself, going through the list of albums.

Donnie stops and double clicks on a picture of Ike up on stage in front of thousands of people, and a list of more pictures expand from the same night. Donnie scrolls through, looking for a specific picture. "Bingo." Donnie says, double clicking on a selfie of Ike and him sitting in a booth.

Donnie zooms into the graying but brown headed man and a younger, scrawny guy, sitting at the table behind them. Donnie prints the picture, and goes onto look for another picture. There is a knock at his front door, and Donnie looks up. Donnie closes the laptop and walks down the hall. Grabbing the printed picture off the printer in the living room, as he walks toward the door.

There is another loud bang at the door, and Donnie opens it. There stands Britt who steps in and pushes the door closed. Before she does, Donnie sees a small crowd of people out on the sidewalk. "What are you doing here?" Donnie asks, turning toward Britt.

"You ditched me at the gas station." Britt says, shaking her head.

"You drive a sports car like a girl." Donnie says, sticking out his tongue out, goofy. "So how did you find me?"

"Forget you have an alarm?" Britt says raising her eyebrows with a laugh.

"Oh was that the beeping sound? God it was annoying." Donnie says, laughing afterwards.

"Well, I'm not the only one who found you." Britt says, nodding to the people outside.

"Who is the entourage?" Donnie says, looking out his curtains by the front door.

Britt pulls out her phone, and pulls up a video White texted to her. She hits play. "You learn, you grow, you fall, you hurt." The skinny, half-naked female, says behind the man in Donnie's picture he is still holding.

The woman slaps the back of the naked and injured man strapped upwards on a metal platform. "Find Donnie, and hurt him." The man says, and the video ends.

"What t-"

"Those people aren't here because they want to stand there." Britt says, as Donnie peaks back out his window and sees about a dozen people standing around his yard and at the end of his driveway.

"Who is that man in the video?" Donnie asks, trying to ignore the sight of Ike getting slapped.

" I don't know." Britt replies.

"I do." Donnie says, handing her the picture he was holding in his hand.

Donnie points to the side profile of the graying, brown haired man sitting in the picture. "He was in Colorado." Donnie explains. "And that guy."

Donnie points to the younger blonde guy, sitting across from the man. "Looks offly familiar to-"

Donnie pauses and opens the curtains, and points to the guy in the street. "That guy."

"Let me call it-"

"No we do this my way, we aren't losing him." Donnie says, pulling open the door. "Yeah, I can't wait for the concert. It's gonna be fun!" Donnie says, looking back at Britt, who follows him out.

"You're just looking forward to partying." Britt says, laughing and playing along with Donnie's plan.

"Can you blame me?" Donnie asks, walking to the driver's door of his truck.

The crowd starts approaching them, as Donnie fakes struggling with his truck's keys. The target gets close to Donnie, and Donnie finally gets his door open, monitoring the crowd approaching. "No I can't. Partying makes it fun." Britt says, opening her door, as the crowd gets to Donnie.

One guy grabs Donnie's arm and the others push him against the truck. The blonde guy from the picture pulls out a video camera, and starts filming as the crowd tries to overpower Donnie. No one pays attention to Britt, allowing her to sneak toward the guy with the camera. "What's going on?" Donnie asks, acting like he doesn't know why they are here.

"We have to save David!" A older lady says, as Donnie fights the two guys trying to pin his arms.

Britt gets to the guy with the camera, and he looks up, seeing her. He goes to run, but Britt quickly grabs his shoulder and arm, throwing him to the ground. "If you want to save him, I'm trying to do the same." Donnie says, trying to talk the crowd down, as punches start flying at him.

A guy punches Donnie in the stomach, causing him to cringe just slightly. "He's telling the truth." Britt says, sweat rolling down her cheeks from continuing to wrestle the guy, who is lying under her. "David is his best friend!"

The same black haired, meat head, punches Donnie again. "That guy over there knows where he is." Donnie says, trying to get out of the guy's hands.

The black haired guy punches Donnie again, right below the ribs. "He's lying." The guy says, determined to cause Donnie pain. "We have to save David!"

"From who?" Donnie asks, as the guy knees him in the stomach.

The crowd, other than the two guys holding his arms and the guy punching him, stands there, confused looking at Donnie. "I have been trying to find him, plea-"

The guy punches Donnie again, interrupting him. "Stop!" yells a lady, pulling the black-haired guy away from Donnie, who is coughing. "We should listen to him."

The two guys wrestle with Donnie for a few more seconds, before Donnie pushes them off of him. As Donnie goes to walk away from his truck, the black haired guy comes back, and punches him in the cheek. Donnie stumbles back, not expecting the hit, holding onto his truck to regain his composure. The crowd grabs the meat head away from Donnie. "Chill out!" The red shirted guy, who was holding one of Donnie's arms says, as the guy tries to get out of the crowd's grasp.

Donnie regains his composure and walks toward Britt, who is kneed on the back of the guy. Donnie steps on the guy's back, and offers Britt help up. Donnie yanks the guy to his feet by the hair on the back of his head, as the crowd approaches him. The guy starts fighting and trying to break Donnie's grasp on the back of his head, as Donnie turns the man toward him. The two guys who were holding Donnie to his truck grabs the scrawny guy's arms. "I will give you one change." Donnie says, trying to contain his anger, knowing this guy may be the only way he will find his best friend. "Where the hell is Ike?"

"Who is Ike?" The guy says, struggling to get out of the grip of the two guys holding him tight.

The meathead who was punching Donnie, walks up behind the guy, and grabs his shirt, lifting him onto his tiptoes, as Donnie punches the guy in the face. "Want to give that one more try?" Donnie asks, as the guy spits blood onto the ground.

"I don't know wh-"

Donnie punches the guy in the stomach. "Don't make me hurt you, kid." Donnie says, as the guy coughs, blood now dripping from his nose.

"Who -"

Donnie goes to swing again and Britt grabs his arm. "Do you recognize this man?" Britt asks, holding up the picture of the guys in the booth that Donnie printed.

"That's my boss." The blonde haired, twenty year old says.

"Where can I find this boss?" Donnie asks, pissed.

"I don't know." The twenty-year old says, and Donnie punches him again.

"I don't want to know that you don't know, tell me what you do know!" Donnie yells, getting into the guy's face.

"Please," the blonde haired, young man says, crying.

Donnie grabs the kid's face, and Britt grabs his arm. "You better speak, or you'll have something to beg for." Donnie says, throwing the guy's head to the side.

"He never tells me his name, but he contacts me via text message with tasks he wants me to complete." The kid says, through tears.

"Where is his office?" Britt asks, Donnie still in the kid's face.

"I don-"

Donnie gets closer and the kid hides his face. "He doesn't have an office. He doesn't have a location, he likes being mobile." The kid says, tears rolling down his cheeks, as he is terrified that Donnie is going to hurt him.

"Where can we find him?" Britt asks.

"I only have a number." the kid says, handing Donnie his phone. "Last number."

Donnie backs away from the kid and shows Britt the kid's phone, and she writes it down on her notebook. She walks away pulling out her phone and calling Kyle. "Hey can you run a number for me?" Britt asks, when Kyle answers the phone.

Donnie walks back to kid, who is now being held by only the meathead who punched Donnie. Donnie bends down into his ankle and grabs his handgun out. "Get in the truck." Donnie says, and the meat head lets go of Tyler.

Tyler freezes, and Donnie walks toward him, and he quickly walks toward the truck. Donnie follows him, and Tyler goes to get in the back seat. "No Driver's seat." Donnie says, and Tyler goes to the front door, getting in.

The three men who are still left from the large crowd that had gathered for Donnie walks up. "Need help?" The guy in the red sweatshirt asks, as Donnie closes the driver's door on his truck.

"We're good." Donnie says, knowing it's going to be dangerous and doesn't want to endanger the guys.

"Perfect." The guy in the red shirt opens the back door and jumps into Donnie's truck, his friend following right behind him.

Britt walks up, as Donnie looks a little shocked that the guys got into the truck. "Are they on their way?" Donnie asks, as the back door closes.

Britt nods. "Stay here, gotta grab something in the house." Donnie says, running back toward the house.

Donnie runs inside and to his room, opening his closet. In his closet is a large safe with a keypad to open. Donnie enters the four digit number, and opens it, exposing seven large firearms. "Need help?" Britt asks, scaring Donnie who jumps and turns toward her.

"Did you leave him out there?" Donnie asks, worried he's gonna run away.

"The guys are watching him." Britt says, taking three of the guns from Donnie, who grabs a couple extra mags for each gun.

Donnie jumps up slamming the safe shut. Donnie leads Britt back to the truck, and both jump in. "Let's do this." Donnie says, pulling out the Tyler's phone, and dialing the number.

"What are you doing?" Tyler asks, looking over at Donnie, worried.

"Do you have him?" A deep male voice asks, coldly.

Donnie nods toward Tyler. "Yes sir. Him and his girlfriend." Tyler responds, acting calm.

"Alive?" the deep male voice asks.

"Yes sir. Badly beaten, but should be alive enough to play." Tyler says, and Donnie nods.

"Fantastic. Meet me at the game room." The deep male voice says, emotionless.

"Yes sir." Tyler says, and Donnie hangs up the phone.

"What's the address for the game room?" Britt asks, Tyler, who's eyes are looking straight at the road.

"I can-"

Donnie slams his hand on the dashboard, making Tyler jump.

"Fifth and Turner." Tyler says, quivering.

Donnie nods, sitting back in his seat, trying to keep his mind clear of the emotions, but failing. Donnie begins to think about Ike, and what he will do if he finds him. What if he's dead? He was pretty beaten up at the time of the videos, who says he isn't dead? Donnie shakes his head shaking off the thought of losing his best friend. "Good, now drive." Donnie says, pointing a black and white Glock handgun at Tyler, who puts the truck in reverse.

Chapter 24

The warmth takes over my body, as the hits come.
"Ike." Kerra's voice says, sternly.

I tried. I can't do it. I can't make it. "I know
baby." Kerra says, less worried or pained as I would
expect.

I sit there, on what looks like a cliff. Kerra is
standing behind me, but walks up to me and sits down
next to me. I'm sorry Kerra. I've tried, but I just can't do
it. I'm not strong enough. The pain is too much.

I feel her hand wrap around my shoulder, and I
tremble at the comforting feeling of her hand. I miss you
baby. I want to be with you. I want to take you to Paris.

"I know baby. But we will do that when I come
join you." Kerra says, as I look down below my feet to
see nothing, but darkness.

Join me where?

"Down there." Kerra says, and I feel her
hand push me from behind. I try to catch myself as my
body slides over the edge of the cliff.

KERRA! I try to grab her leg, but she is no
longer there. Help! Don't do this!

The area around me turns black and suddenly all the pain I am in comes back to me. My body goes limp, and I can no longer scream or move. I land quickly on a hard object.

Wait no, I am hit by a hard object. My body doesn't move. It is numb and limp. My head hangs, and my eyelids stay shut. "It's really terrible, that I have to do this." The head honcho says, swinging another time, hitting me in the back. "Had the other players been strong enough, you wouldn't be here."

I can't cough. I can't move. I can't breathe. I just lay there limp, as he hits me continuously with the baseball bat. "I wonder if Donnie will be strong enough." The king sadist says, hitting me in the leg with the baseball bat. "What about his girlfriend?"

Donnie? Britt? Dating? What? Are they coming? Is Donnie okay? Are they okay?

I cannot move, all I can do is think, but even that is hard to do, as my head's splitting with pain. Another hit to my head, and all thoughts stop. I just lay there motionless. "Ike." I hear Kerra say. "I'll join you soon."

She's telling me I can move on, but I don't want to. I can't leave her by herself. I can't leave her. "You don't have a choice." Kerra says, coldly. "You're not strong enough to survive."

I am. I can. "No you can't." Kerra says. "You're going to die."

Another hit to my head and I feel my consciousness slipping away. I have fought hard. I have played the game. Some games are not winnable. "You're going to die." Kerra repeats, and it echoes through my head as another hit hits the back of my skull.

My hope of survival vanishes, as more hits hit me. "Black truck getting close to the property."

Black truck? Donnie has a black truck.

"Let it come." The boss man says, as there is another hit on my back.

I'm not going to survive. I can't do this. It's time to call the end of the game. I'm not strong enough. I take a breath and it is interrupted by a lack of consciousness.

I won't survive this. Kerra, I love you.

Chapter 25

Donnie is sitting in the front passenger seat, while Alex, Brock, and Britt are sitting in the back, all holding firearms. No one says a word.

"They will kill you and me." Tyler says, stiffly, his knuckles white around the steering wheel while his eyes are locked on the road.

"Not before I kill every single one of them." Donnie says, not intimidated by Tyler or his threats.

"He won't stop till he gets what he wants." Tyler says, his voice cold and filled with fear that he tries to hard to hide.

"And what's that?" Alex, in the back seat says.

"To find someone strong enough to win." Tyler says, with a smirk. "It's all a game to him. Six levels or doors, all worst than the last."

Donnie glances back at Britt, both sharing the same look of worry for Ike and what he has had to endure. "How far out are we?" Donnie asks, ignoring the kid's comment. "I want to be that person, and show him how to win the game without playing."

Tyler shakes his head. "Two minutes." Tyler says, a cold sweat sitting on his forehead.

Donnie racks his handgun, and Tyler cringes. "If he wants a game I'll give him a game."

"Back up is on the way as well." Britt says, trying to remind Donnie that he doesn't have to do this rescue mission by himself.

Donnie looks back at Britt and puts his hand on her leg. "The clean up crew." Donnie says, winking at her, trying to ease her worry.

"Just don't make Ike come home to burying his best friend." Britt says, rubbing Donnie's hand, her hands tense with worry that Donnie is going to do something stupid.

"We are here." Tyler says, looking in the rear view mirror.

Donnie sits forward and shrugs his shoulders. Alex hands up an assault rifle to Donnie, who puts his hand gun in his waist holster before grabbing it. "Let's get this game started!" Donnie exclaims as the car rolls to a start.

Donnie and Alex quickly jump out of the car, but Donnie turns real fast, ducking to the back of his truck as there is several loud bangs from the doorway of the building.

"Boss, he's here!" The same young voice from earlier calls, as several swings of the baseball bat hits David in the back.

"Bring him to me." The boss man says, as David's body hangs limp.

"What should I do with her?" The young voice says, standing in the doorway of the room.

"Her?" The head honcho asks, swinging the baseball bat into David's upper legs.

"His girlfriend." The young helper explains.

The head honcho smiles, and looks toward the young brown headed boy. They lock eyes, and the head honcho says, "Kill her."

The head honcho laughs and swings the baseball bat into the back of David's skull. "Looks like we have your replacement." he says, with a menacing laugh, leaning in toward David's body.

David doesn't move. He doesn't open his eyes. His face is tight, but it doesn't move with the followed hit.

Suddenly there is a series of loud pops from the other room. The boss man looks over at the door, a little weary of the repetitive loud sounds. The pops or gunshots get closer to the door, and he drops the baseball bat, and walks over to the table a few feet away. He grabs his pistol off the table and watches the door, as there is the sound of screaming. The inaudible yelling gets louder as there are several more pops occur. "Oh shit, he's awake." The boss man hears one of his men yell from the other room.

"There's four of them!" Another one yells, as there are more pops from the other room.

"Cops approaching from the north." The voice belonging to the helper who told the boss man about Donnie's truck, says.

The head honcho looks slightly panicked, as the yelling turns to screams of pain and the pops fade into rifle gunshots. He grabs his keys off the table and tries to find the right key. His heart begins to pick up speed, as the gunshots get closer and screams continue. He struggles to unlock the locks on David's wrists and ankles.

The head honcho, finally showing weakness, drops his keys because of his worry and anxiety. He picks them up and unlocks David's last lock, releasing his body to fall to the ground. The gunshots occur right outside the door. "OPEN IT!" The head honcho hears an authoritative male voice yell.

He grabs David around the neck and pushes the gun to the right temple of his bruised, battered, and broken skull. More gunshots occur followed by rattling on the doorknob. The boss man becomes extremely panicked, and looks for a good hiding spot. With a wide open room, except the platform David was strapped to, he begins to panic. "I will kill him!" He yells, as the rustling and gunshots continue to occur right outside of the door.

"Boss, it's just me." The warning voice from before says, as there is more rattling at the door.

"Don't come in!" The boss man yells, knowing it's not just his worker on the other side of that door.

"Let me in." The warning voice says, as there is another gunshot.

The sounds go silent, and that just makes the boss man's anxiety worst. "If you come in here, I will kill him!" He yells, trying to scare off the person he knows is standing on the other side of the door.

The head honcho turns the gun toward the door. There is a huge flash of light and a large bang as the door swings wide open. The head honcho shoos the mass, sitting in the doorway. The smaller human like mass falls to the ground, as four more masses make quick entry into the room. The boss man starts shooting, as the room fills with smoke. There is a series of several gunshots from both sides. "Police!" A voice yells, hidden by smoke, as the gunshots stop.

"Ike!" Donnie yells, coughing and weak. "Ike, where are you?"

As the smoke clears out of the room, Donnie is exposed, bent down, dazed. He is looking frantically for his best friend, his mind confused and his emotions even worse. Donnie slides on the floor, his body covered in blood. "IKE!" Donnie says, coughing, and looking up in pain.

Donnie finds a limp body on the ground, naked. Still dazed, he grabs the body, frantically, trying to identify it. "Ike?" Donnie asks, his eyes dazed.

Donnie tries to hold onto the body, but White grabs his arm and pulls him out of the room quickly. Donnie fights, but three officers grab him and pull him off of the floor, away from a limp body. Donnie screams, inaudibly as there is a bunch of noise around him. Tears stream down his face as he tries to make it back into the room. The officers finally pull him out of the room and out to Britt. "Let me in there!" Donnie says, as the officer grabs the Glock from Donnie's hand. "Ike!"

Donnie fights, and Britt grabs him. "Donnie."

"Ike!" Donnie yells, trying to get out of Britt's grip.

The officers wrestle with Donnie, and Kerra comes running up. She goes to run inside, but sees the officers stopping Donnie. Tears rolling down her face, she turns, and pushes her way between the officers. "Donnie. Donnie." Kerra says, grabbing him.

"He's here. Let me save him." Donnie says, crying. "Please."

Donnie fights a few more seconds, but the officers pull him over to a bench. Tears stream down Britt's, Kerra's, and Donnie's faces. Firefighters rush by, as Donnie looks up at Britt, who is standing right in front of him, bent down. Britt looks at Donnie, and watches as tears roll down from his eyes, and blood drips from his red stained hands, down to his fingertips. She puts her hand on his shoulder, and he begins sobbing. The sky around Donnie begins to fade to orange, and Donnie hangs his head.

Six drops of blood roll off of Donnie's fingertips, as he moves his blood soaked hands to his face. Donnie sits there, still and filled with emotions, as he watches blurs of officers and firefighters run between the building and the vehicles. Donnie squeezes his eyes shut, as tears slip down his blood stained cheeks, and the noises of the chaos turn to silence.